DT

KING OF DEATH

Bruno Scaglia, an animal of a man with the strength of ten, was the king of crime in San Francisco. Now his huge fingers were around Skye Fargo's throat, squeezing.

Bucking like a mustang, Fargo fought to break loose. But he couldn't get enough leverage. Bit by bit the life was being choked from his body. He rained blows, but he might as well have been hitting solid granite.

Then Fargo's fingers closed on a smooth, slender object. He did not need to look to know what it was. Raising it, he sheared the blade into Scaglia's neck just under the jaw. The terror of the Barbary Coast shrieked like a mountain lion and staggered away, tottering toward the door, a red geyser streaming in his wake.

The killer king was dead, Fargo thought with satisfaction, even as Scaglia's men poured through the door. The trouble was, in a minute, the Trailsman would be, too. . . .

Be sure to read the other books in this exciting Trailsman series!

**FROM SPUR AWARD-WINNING
WESTERN WRITER**

SUZANN LEDBETTER

REDEMPTION TRAIL

From her con-man father, Abigail Fiske inherits a stake in a Colorado gold mine. The trail west is treacherous, and when Abigail arrives, she must convince a band of surly prospectors they need a woman in their ranks.

With skills ranging from ledgering to medicine to swinging a rifle, Abigail is up to the task. She braves the pitiless Rockies, squares off with hostile Indians, and weathers the fires of civil war. She even wins the trust and the heart of Garrett Collingsworth, the leader of her prospecting band. But for the greatest prize of all, more dazzling than any cache of ore, Abigail will have to enter a battle only she can fight—and win.

"Suzann Ledbetter is an author to watch."—Terry C. Johnston

from **SIGNET**

THE TRAILSMAN
173

WASHINGTON
WARPATH

by

Jon Sharpe

A SIGNET BOOK

SIGNET
Published by the Penguin Group
Penguin Books USA Inc., 375 Hudson Street,
New York, New York 10014, U.S.A.
Penguin Books Ltd, 27 Wrights Lane,
London W8 5TZ, England
Penguin Books Australia Ltd, Ringwood,
Victoria, Australia
Penguin Books Canada Ltd, 10 Alcorn Avenue,
Toronto, Ontario, Canada M4V 3B2
Penguin Books (N.Z.) Ltd, 182–190 Wairau Road,
Auckland 10, New Zealand

Penguin Books Ltd, Registered Offices:
Harmondsworth, Middlesex, England

First published by Signet, an imprint of Dutton Signet,
a division of Penguin Books USA Inc.

First Printing, May, 1996
10 9 8 7 6 5 4 3 2 1

The first chapter of this book previously appeared in *Sutter's Secret*,
the one hundred seventy-second volume in this series.

REGISTERED TRADEMARK—MARCA REGISTRADA

Printed in the United States of America

The Trailsman

Beginnings . . . they bend the tree and they mark the man. Skye Fargo was born when he was eighteen. Terror was his midwife, vengeance his first cry. Killing spawned Skye Fargo, ruthless, cold-blooded murder. Out of the acrid smoke of gunpowder still hanging in the air, he rose, cried out a promise never forgotten.

The Trailsman they began to call him all across the West: searcher, scout, hunter, the man who could see where others only looked, his skills for hire but not his soul, the man who lived each day to the fullest, yet trailed each tomorrow. Skye Fargo, the Trailsman, and the seeker who could take the wildness of a land and the wanting of a woman and make them his own.

1860. The remote region around Mount Saint Helens— where few white men had ever been and lived to tell about it . . .

1

Skye Fargo liked San Francisco.

At night a man could go for a stroll through the Barbary Coast district and run into more lovely ladies of the night on each block than he would encounter in entire cities back East. Tall ones, short ones, skinny ones, plump ones—most dressed in skimpy outfits that would get them arrested if they dared show their cleavage in places like Omaha or Pittsburgh or Cincinnati. Redheads, blondes, brunettes, and raven-haired doves were there for the asking, and the right price.

It made Fargo's head swim to see so much natural beauty parading around like fillies at a stud farm.

The heady scent of mingled perfumes was downright intoxicating. All the big man with the lake-blue eyes had to do was turn a different direction and another wafting fragrance tingled his nostrils. It was like being in a flower shop, only better.

Skye Fargo was going to treat himself. He had spent the past week carrying a dispatch for the Army from Carson City to the coast. Along the way he'd had to evade uppity Paiutes, convince a mountain lion that his horse would make a lousy meal, and blow the head off a rattler trying to turn his leg into a pincushion. He deserved a night of fun and frolic.

So far, though, Fargo had not set eyes on the right woman. Several had appealed to him in one way or another, but none had caused that telltale twitching in his loins that told him that they would do to spend the night with.

Fargo liked a certain carefree quality in his females. He wanted a beauty with a sparkle in her eyes and a genuine zest

9

for life, one who would be all over him like a bear on honey and would wear him out with her under-the-covers antics.

Then the Trailsman saw her.

A striking blonde stood on the corner of Kearny Street. Her dress, if you could call it that, was made from the sheerest fabric the big man had ever seen. It covered her from chin to ankles, yet clearly revealed every square inch of her feminine charms underneath. The fact that she was wearing no underclothes at all except for lacy panties helped.

But it was the woman's attitude and posture more than her outrageous attire that made Fargo stop. Her smooth features were crinkled in a friendly smile and she held herself tall and proud. Her back resting on the brick wall of an office building, she gazed at every man who went by, her frank invitation as plain as the cherry-red lips on her face.

Fargo saw her glance at him, saw her blink and stiffen as if in surprise. Hooking his thumbs in his belt, he strolled over and remarked, "Never move to Denver. You'd freeze to death in two seconds wearing an outfit like that."

"Thanks for the advice, handsome," the blonde responded playfully in a sultry voice that brought a lump to Fargo's throat. She studied him from head to toe. "Buckskins and boots and spurs. Something tells me that you're not from around here."

"Only staying the night," Fargo said, "and I'm looking for some company. You interested?"

"The name is Greta." She straightened and stood so close to him that his chest nearly brushed her ample bosom. "Yes, I am. What did you have in mind?"

"A hot meal, a few drinks, and a room at the finest hotel in this part of town," Fargo detailed. "Since you must know San Francisco a lot better than I do, I'll let you be my guide."

Grinning, Greta went to take Fargo's arm, but she froze when her eyes drifted over his shoulder. Pivoting on a heel, Fargo discovered a lean, sallow man crossing the street toward them. Grubby clothes covered the newcomer's lanky frame, and his hair had been slicked back with grease. Fargo took an instant dislike to him.

"There you are, damn it!" the ratty man hailed the blonde. "Bruno had me lookin' all over for you, Greta. He wants to see you right this minute."

The woman's cheeks flushed with annoyance. "I'm not his dog, Wenckus. I don't come running every time he whistles. You go tell him that I'm busy, that I'll be there when I'm good and ready."

Wenckus made a clucking sound. "Tell him yourself, gorgeous. You know as well as I do that he's liable to pop a cork. And I'm not takin' the heat. So let's get going." Grasping her wrist, he started to walk off, but Greta wouldn't budge. "Didn't you hear me?" he growled. "Bruno wants you *now*."

Fargo had heard enough. It was plain the woman didn't care to oblige, and he was eager to go fill his belly with a heaping plate of lobster and shrimp. He liked seafood but rarely had an opportunity to indulge himself. Taking a step, he put his hand on the man's arm and said forcefully, "You heard the lady, mister. Let her be."

Wenckus jerked his arm loose and hissed like a riled sidewinder. "Who the hell are you? Didn't your pa ever tell you it's bad manners to stick your nose where it doesn't belong? Get lost, hick, before I decide to carve you up into little pieces."

Fargo hit him. He flicked a quick jab that staggered the ratty man backward. Wenckus dug in his feet, swayed, shook his head, and touched the trickle of blood seeping from the left corner of his mouth.

"Damn you, you bastard! I'll kill you for this!"

A knife blade flashed in the dim light. Fargo crouched as Wenckus came at him. He dodged a wild swing, ducked a low swipe. Enraged, Wenckus thrust, overextending himself, and Fargo seized the man's arm, slammed his knee into the elbow, and heard a gratifying snap. It provoked a screech of sheer agony. The knife clattered to the walk and Wenckus pressed his clipped wing to his side.

"Son of a bitch!"

"Maybe now you'll take the hint," Fargo suggested. Gripping Greta's elbow, he turned to depart, keeping one eye on the shifty rodent. He was glad he did.

Uttering a high-pitched shriek, Wenckus launched himself at Fargo, kicking out with a heavy black boot. He aimed the blow at Fargo's spine but the big man danced out of harm's way, shifted, and delivered an uppercut that lifted Wenckus off his feet and sent him crashing onto his back a few feet away. Groaning, the man attempted to sit up. Fargo cocked his leg and planted his foot on the tip of Wenckus's jaw. That did the trick.

People had stopped whatever they were doing to stare. A few were hurrying over to see what the fuss was about. Since Fargo had no desire to tangle with the local law, he hastened off with the ravishing blonde at his side. She never said a word until several blocks were behind them.

"You shouldn't have done that, mister."

Fargo shrugged. "The name is Skye. And he was a pain in the ass. I bet people do it to him all the time."

"That's not what I meant. Wenckus works for Bruno Scaglia, and Bruno is not the sort of guy you want to have mad at you. He has an interest in every racket on the Barbary Coast. If he wants someone dead, all he has to do is snap his fingers and they wind up on the bottom of San Francisco Bay."

"Why did you buck him, then?"

Her lovely face clouded. "Bruno thinks I'm his woman. He took a liking to me a while back and hasn't given me a moment's peace ever since, even though I've told him again and again that I don't want to see him. He just can't take no for an answer."

"Forget about him. You're with me tonight, and I'm not about to let anyone spoil our evening. Relax and enjoy yourself."

Greta pursed her lips, chuckled, and nodded. "All right. The least I can do to thank you for sparing me another night of hell with Bruno is treat you to a good time the likes of which you won't ever forget."

"Lead on."

The blonde steered Fargo down to the wharf at the north end of the waterfront. There, in a fancy restaurant decorated with anchors, boat wheels, and even large nets, they were treated to a feast fit for a king. Fargo relished every morsel of juicy lobster and the succulent shrimp meat. He dipped each piece in thick butter before rolling it on his tongue to savor the taste.

His escort watched him in amusement. About halfway through the meal she laughed and declared, "I don't think I've ever seen anyone take so much pleasure in eating before. Are you half-starved?"

Fargo shook his head. "You're looking at a man who gets by on beef, venison, and jerky most of the time. This is a treat for me. And so is this." Picking up the tall glass of wine, he gulped and smacked his lips. "It's not coffin varnish, but I can't complain."

"Coffin varnish?"

"That's how some folks in Texas describe good sipping whiskey. If it can't put a shine on a casket or hair on a frog, it's not worth the bother."

Her gay mirth pealed through the room. "I take it you've seen a lot of the country, Skye."

"More than most," Fargo admitted. At her prompting, he told about some of his wide-flung travels, from the Everglades of Florida to the deep woods of remote Canada, from the arid deserts in Arizona to the pristine peaks of Montana. She listened intently, fascinated, and between the two of them they polished off two bottles of wine and began a third.

The meal made Fargo sluggish. It had been so long since he'd gorged himself that his body did not know how to handle it. The wine, which he regarded as little more than colored water, was more potent than he had counted on. By the third bottle he kept hearing an odd buzz in his ears and he was pleasantly tipsy.

After the big man paid, they ambled out onto a pier and watched the lights of a ship in the distance. A brisk breeze from the northwest fanned Fargo's brow and cooled him down. The sight of Greta, her lush body outlined against the backdrop of tranquil ocean, had the opposite effect. Pulling her close, he touched his lips to hers. They were as soft as silk, as tasty as peaches smothered in sugar. Her smooth tongue glided into his mouth, entwining with his. For all of a minute they were locked in a tight embrace. When they parted, Fargo swore that his blood was pounding a drumbeat in his veins.

"Ummmm. That was nice," Greta said. "I can't wait to get to a hotel."

"Then what are we waiting for?" Fargo responded. He had money to spare, and it was burning a hole in his pocket. Looping an arm around her slender waist, he swiveled toward shore. And promptly froze.

A pair of brawny men stood at the other end of the pier, as if waiting for them.

"Oh, no," Greta said softly. "I knew this would happen. Bruno has eyes and ears everywhere."

Fargo led her toward shore. Since it was against the law for a man to parade around with a pistol strapped to his hip in San Francisco, Fargo had tucked his up under his shirt and wedged it under the belt over his left hip, butt forward for a swift draw. He loosened his shirt now as he approached the burly longshoremen, who moved to bar his path.

"Bruno Scaglia wants to have a word with you, friend," stated the older of the duo. "You and the lady, both. You're to come with us."

"No."

The men exchanged glances and the older one said, "Maybe your ears don't work so good. What Mr. Scaglia wants, Mr. Scaglia gets. Make this easy on yourself." To accent his point, he bunched his ham-sized right fist and smacked it into his calloused left palm with a sharp crack. "Hear that?"

Fargo produced the Colt with a flourish and twirled it forward and back. Suddenly leveling it at the speaker, he cocked the hammer, retorting, "Hear this?"

At the metallic rasp both men tensed. The younger one took a step to the rear and raised both hands, as if to ward off a slug.

"Go tell Mr. Scaglia that the lady and I have other plans," Fargo said coldly. "And let him know that I don't want to be bothered again. I have a short fuse and he's mighty close to setting it off."

The talkative one scowled as he retreated into the night, saying, "This ain't over, mister. Not by a long shot. We'll pass on what you said, but Mr. Scaglia doesn't back down from anyone. You'll see."

Fargo hefted the pistol and smiled as the pair hustled into the darkness. Only when they had rounded a far corner and disappeared did he tuck the six-shooter back under his shirt and cover it. His companion stared at him in wide-eyed wonder.

"Aren't you just full of surprises!" Greta commented. "What are you? A desperado of some kind?"

Resuming their stroll, Fargo answered, "I don't make a habit of breaking the law unless it's a law so stupid it deserves to be broken." He patted his shirt, insuring the revolver was in place. "To make ends meet, at one time or another I've worked as a scout, a wagon train guide, a tracker, and more."

"And you never get an urge to set down roots?"

"Not yet," Fargo said. "I was bit by the wanderlust bug before I turned sixteen. I haven't looked back since."

Greta sighed wistfully. "How I envy you. I wish to high heaven I could do like you—go where I please when I please. It sounds like the kind of life most people would give their eyeteeth to have."

Making small talk, the Trailsman and the dove hiked toward the center of the city. The streets were alive with foot and wagon traffic. San Francisco, he had been told, never slept; the people were on the go twenty-four hours a day. And he believed it. Every so often he checked behind them, but there was no evidence of anyone shadowing them.

"I know an excellent hotel called the Concord House," Greta revealed. "It's pricey, and it should be. They have thick red carpet in each room and big beds and mirrors on the wall. Room service will bring up a three-course meal. And they have the freshest smelling soap in the world."

Fargo gave her bottom a lusty slap. It didn't matter to him where they spent the night. In his view one bed was as good as another. "If that's where you want to go, then the Concord House it is."

They turned into Portsmouth Square, the pulsing hub of San Francisco's gambling resorts, as casinos were commonly called. Although the city fathers were making a lot of noise in the local papers about clamping down on vice, the police seldom bothered to raid a casino, nor had they closed a single one down.

Portsmouth Square was lined with one den of iniquity after another. Prestigious places like the El Dorado and the Bella Donna were known as the cream of the crop. No expense had been spared in turning them into the most splendid establishments of their kind anywhere in the world.

The square was filled with those who favored the city's nightlife. Men in expensive suits mingled with rough miners in dirty flannel shirts and shapeless hats. Mexicans wrapped in serapes leaned against walls, smoking their *cigarrillos*. Women were fewer, but those present were dressed in exquisite dresses that showed off their bodies to perfection.

Skye Fargo found the swirl of activity intoxicating. He was strongly tempted to pay a visit to a poker table, but if he lost his poke he would be unable to afford the deluxe room Greta had her heart set on. As they wound through the stream of humanity, a female voice abruptly squealed Greta's name. From out of the doorway of a gambling hall shot a shapely brunet in a blue dress who threw her arms around the blonde and raved over and over again about how glad she was to see her.

"This is one of my best friends, Blanche Cunnings," Greta explained when the other woman calmed down.

"Pleased to met you, big man," Blanche said, her warm hand lingering in Fargo's much longer than was necessary. "Where has she been hiding you?"

Before Fargo could respond, the two women took to chatting in hushed tones. He tolerated their giggling and their coy looks as long as he could, then she snatched Greta's hand and said, "It was nice to meet you. We have to be going."

"Hold on, Skye," Greta said. "Blanche just invited us to join her party here in the Sacramento. She says the men with her won't mind, and we can have free drinks while we watch them play. What do you say?"

Spending time with a bunch of strangers was the last thing Fargo wanted to do, but he was reluctant to disappoint Greta. As if she could read his thoughts, she squeezed his hand and pecked him on the cheek.

"Please? For me? We won't be long. I promise. It's just that I haven't seen her in weeks, and we have catching up to do."

"Just so the free drinks are whiskey," Fargo grumbled, and nodded. The women pounced on him as if he were the prize at a raffle drawing and whisked him indoors. Right away a smoky haze enveloped them, and the strong scent of alcohol filled the air. So did the murmur of subdued talk that rose from the scores of players lining the tables along both walls and the hordes of onlookers packing the open spaces in between. There were so many people that it was a chore to elbow through to the faro table where the brunet's three refined friends wanted to play. None of the trio gave Fargo more than a casual glance.

Fargo did not stay there long. The women were huddled to one side, ignoring him, so he shouldered his way to the bar and was waited on by a portly man in a white apron. His first sip of the whiskey sparked a contented sigh. It was the genuine article, not the watered down excuse for red-eye that many places sold.

Facing the room, Fargo leaned his elbows on the edge of the counter and idly observed all that was going on. The most popular game was without a doubt faro, in which players bet on the value of cards as the dealers exposed them. At a table near him, a man bet a stack of chips six inches high and never blinked an eye when he lost and the dealer raked them in.

A commotion broke out near the entrance. Half a dozen men had entered and were barreling their way through the crowd. In their lead was a mountain of a man, as tall as he was wide, dressed in the very best suit money could buy. Gold rings glittered on each finger, and he wore a gold watch chain as thick as a rope. Trailing him were two familiar faces: the longshoremen.

17

Instantly Fargo set down his whiskey and moved to intercept the hulking leader before the man reached Greta. He got there, but only a few steps ahead. The women were so busy gossiping that they hadn't noticed. Planting his feet wide, he declared, "You must be Scaglia."

The criminal kingpin regarded the Trailsman as if he were a bug fit to be squashed. "And you must be the son of a bitch who thinks he can get off with telling me what to do. Well, I'm here to show you the error of your ways, boy."

Fargo had his shirt tucked in. It would be impossible for him to unlimber the Colt before the roughnecks plowed into him. Trying to avoid trouble, he forced himself to stay calm and said, "I'm just looking to have a good time with the lady here. All we want is to be left in peace."

"Fat chance," Bruno Scaglia snapped, his fleshy cheeks and double chin quivering with fury. He swung the long, polished cane in his right hand. As he did, there was a click.

A blade four inches long popped out of the tapered end, spearing at Fargo's throat. Only a desperate twist spared Fargo's life. He batted the cane aside, stepped in close, and delivered a solid punch to Scaglia's gut. It was like striking solid rock. His knuckles flared with pain.

Incredibly, the kingpin laughed, a low, rumbling sound like the snarling of a great bear. "Did you think that would hurt me, little man? Before I came to California and made my mark gambling, I used to work in a quarry in Ohio. From dawn to dusk six days a week, I lifted boulders bigger than you. Ask anyone. You couldn't hurt me if you tried."

"Then you won't hold it against me if I make a liar out of you?" Fargo replied, even as he lifted his right boot and brought the heel down with all his might on the tip of Scaglia's left shoe.

The man's roar stopped every game in the gambling hall and drew all eyes to the towering figure, who had lifted his hurt foot just as Fargo unleashed a roundhouse right that caught Bruno Scaglia on the right cheek and tottered him back into a table. The legs were unable to support his massive bulk. With a rending crash, kingpin and table smashed to the floor.

Scaglia floundered up and bellowed at his stunned men, "What the hell are you waiting for? *Nail the bastard!*"

The longshoremen were quick to obey. Lunging, they tackled Fargo as he tried to skip aside. Fargo winched as a fist caught him in the ribs. Another glanced off his chin. He was able to partly turn as he fell so that he wound up on his side with only one man on top of him. An elbow to the nose knocked the roughneck off. The second one drew back a fist, but Fargo slammed his forehead into the longshoreman's face, then rolled backward out of reach.

For a few moments Fargo was in the clear. Out of the corner of one eye he saw a gambler rise to protest the intrusion and be slammed flat by one of Scaglia's men. Another gambler leaped to the defense of the first and another of Scaglia's cutthroats entered the fray. In a twinkling a dozen more men piled in, and the room erupted in savage violence.

Fargo lost sight of Greta and Blanche. The swirling melee also hid Bruno Scaglia. Thinking that he could get out of there without anyone being the wiser, he rose onto his hands and knees and started to crawl toward the bar. The next moment a shadow fell across him, and he looked up to see a man in miner's clothes holding a chair overhead. "Now hold on," he said. "I'm not to blame—"

It was a waste of breath. The last sight Fargo saw was the chair sweeping down toward his head. Then a keg of black powder exploded in his skull and a black cloud claimed his shattered senses.

2

Skye Fargo felt as if his skull had been split down the middle. He revived slowly, flooded with pain so intense it made him grit his teeth. An awful smell caused his stomach to do flip-flops.

Someone groaned, and Fargo realized it was he himself. Cracking his eyes open, he squinted in the harsh glare of sunlight streaming in through a barred window high on a wall across the small room in which he found himself. He was on his back in a low bunk that creaked as he sat up and looked around.

"Welcome back to the world of the living, friend," said one of five nattily dressed men who also occupied the jail cell. "We wagered on when you would come around, and I've won. I knew you were a tough jasper."

The men were gamblers. Fargo nodded at them, then grimaced when the simple motion aggravated his torment. He swung his legs over the side of the bunk, nearly gagging as the terrible stink grew stronger. "What is that damn smell?" he muttered.

A man fiddling with a pair of dice pointed at a bunk above Fargo's. "I believe that gentleman can answer your question."

Straightening, Fargo discovered an elderly man in tattered clothes and worn shoes who was curled into a ball, snoring lightly. He reeked of alcohol, and worse. The contents of his stomach had been strewn over his shirt, over his pants, and over a sizable portion of the bunk. "Why doesn't the jailer clean this mess?" he asked, backing away from the stench with a hand over his mouth.

The gambler with the dice snickered. "Sergeant Harve Taylor thinks its hilarious that we have to sit in here and suffer. He won't clean it until he's damn good and ready."

Fargo reached up. His hat was perched at a slant on his matted hair. The chair had split his skin and he had bled freely but apparently not for very long. A knot the size of a hen's egg marked the spot. Just touching it sent a pang shooting through him.

"I'd take it easy for a while, mister," said the same cardsharp handling the dice. "Captain Baker had a sawbones in to look at you. The doc said you'd live, but you wouldn't be doing any yodeling for a spell."

"Yodeling?" Fargo repeated.

"You know. Over in Germany or Switzerland or some such place, people like to climb to the tops of the mountains and shout their names to hear the echo. That's called yodeling."

Fargo wasn't so sure the gambler was right, but he was not about to quibble, the shape he was in. Besides, he could hardly care less. "How long—?" he began.

"Have you been out?" the gambler finished for him. "Well, let's see. They brought us in here about midnight last night, and it's close to two in the afternoon now, so you've been lying there at least fourteen hours." He offered his hand. "Bill Bridge is the name, Lady Luck my game. As you've no doubt gathered."

Fargo shook lightly and eased into a squat. "Where exactly are we?"

"The Fourth Precinct jailhouse," Bridge revealed. "The wagons brought us here after the raid." He grinned when Fargo let his confusion show. "The raid on the Sacramento. Some damn fool started a fight, and the next thing, practically every idiot in the place was taking a swing at someone else. I bet most of the furniture was smashed to pieces." Bridge sighed. "The owner sent a runner to the police and within five minutes the place was swarming with coppers. Men were bailing out of windows, trying to get away. It was a regular madhouse."

Fargo remembered none of it. Naturally, his Colt was gone, but so was his poke.

Bridge noticed him grope his pants. "Sorry, stranger. They take everything." Chuckling, he wagged the dice. "Well, almost everything. I keep these hidden in a secret compartment in my shoe."

A rumble from Fargo's stomach reminded him that it had been over twenty-four hours since he ate last. "Do they ever feed us?" he wondered aloud.

"Twice a day. Swill for breakfast, and warm swill for supper." Bridge smiled broadly, displaying a tiny inlaid diamond in one of his upper front teeth. "I recommend the cuisine heartily."

Fargo would have laughed, only he knew how much it would hurt. A cough to the left alerted him to the fact that there were five adjoining cells, and each contained six to ten men, most wearing the trademark apparel of professional gamblers: black suits, white ruffled shirts, and high silk hats. A few had fur-collared capes draped over their shoulders. All wore looks of utter boredom.

"You've noticed how many of my peers are present? There's a reason," Bridge commented. "Our fraternity has an understanding with the police. They don't make trouble for us if we keep their pockets lined with cash, and we had better not make any trouble for them in return. When we do, they lock up as many of us as they can get their hands on to teach us a lesson."

"So what now?" Fargo asked.

"Oh, any time now we'll be taken before a magistrate and fined for disturbing the peace. They've already removed over half of those arrested. By tonight I expect to be back plying my trade."

No sooner were the words out of the gambler's mouth than a thickset sergeant waddled up to the cell door and inserted a massive key. "All right, you lowlifes. Time to see Judge Rodgers."

Bill Bridge stood. As if by magic, his dice had vanished. On hearing the magistrate's name, he moaned and said softly to Fargo, "We're in for it, I'm afraid. Rodgers is one mean son of

22

a bitch. His fines are twice as high as those of any other judge."

In single file the prisoners were ushered down a long, dimly lit hall, through a swinging door into a wider corridor, and finally into a spacious chamber lined with mahogany paneling. On the bench sat a stern white-haired man with weathered features. He regarded the knot of gamblers with disdain.

The proceedings went swiftly. Each gambler took his turn and was fined anywhere from two to six hundred dollars.

Fargo was puzzled by the higher fines for some, until he noticed that those who were polite to Judge Rodgers were given lower amounts, while those who acted as if they held the court in contempt were given a stiffer penalty. Bill Bridge was right before him. The gambler acted as humble as a devout churchgoer and only had to pay one hundred and fifty dollars. On his way out, Bridge winked at Fargo.

Then Rodgers smacked his gravel hard and barked, "Who's next? Don't keep me waiting. If I'm late for my supper, there will be hell to pay."

Quickly taking his place before the bench, Fargo clasped his hands and looked up.

"Name?"

"Skye Fargo."

Judge Rodgers adjusted his spectacles and leaned forward to see better. "So you're him? Funny, you don't look like so much to me."

Not having any idea what the man was talking about, Fargo said, "Your honor, I—"

"Silence, boy!" Rodgers cracked, slamming the gavel again. "You'll talk when I say you can, and not before. Is that clear?"

Fargo nodded.

"I can't hear you."

"Yes, sir," Fargo said calmly. He refused to let his anger get the better of him. For all he knew, the cantankerous cuss might toss him behind bars for six months or longer.

The judge drummed his fingers. "So you're the one who caused this whole mess, are you?"

Flabbergasted, Fargo blurted, "No. Who told you that? It was a man named—"

Scarlet with indignation, Rodgers sprang to his feet and shook the gavel. "Don't lie to me, son! I can read as well if not better than the next man! You're in enough hot water as it is without making matters worse." Struggling to regain his composure, he smoothed his robes and sat back down. "I would imagine that the owner of the Sacramento will be getting in touch with you soon. Or his lawyers. Over a thousand dollars in damage was done, and someone has to foot the bill."

Fargo couldn't keep quiet. "But I'm not to blame, damn it! And I have witnesses who—"

Once more the magistrate leaped erect. For a second it appeared as if he would hurl the gavel, but he gave a mighty shake of his whole body and leaned on the edge of the bench instead. "Profanity in my court! How dare you, sir!" Nodding at the court clerk, he said, "Your fine is set at five hundred dollars. Pay him on your way out."

"I don't have that much money," Fargo said, refusing to be brow-beaten. Trying to pacify the old coot was a lost cause.

"How much *do* you have?"

"Two hundred. That is, if the police will give me back my poke."

Judge Rodgers glanced at Sergeant Taylor. "Harve, did you confiscate a poke from this gentleman?"

The thickset policeman never batted an eye. "No, sir. All we took from him was a pistol hidden under his shirt and a knife stuck down in his boot."

"What?" Rodgers exclaimed, and consulted the papers in front of him. "Why, mercy me. I never even noticed the charge of carrying concealed weapons. This puts everything in a whole new light." Grinning like a cat about to swallow a goldfish, the magistrate entwined his fingers and said with mock humility, "It pains me to have to say this, young man, but you are a detriment to our fair city and our illustrious nation."

"What?" Fargo couldn't believe his ears.

"Vagabonds like you cause nothing but trouble wherever they go. Take yourself, for example. You waltz into San Francisco, defy our firearms ordinance, associate with ladies of ill repute, cause a near riot, and then have the unmitigated gall to accuse our fine police force of stealing your money." Rodgers sadly shook his head. "Your fine for disturbing the peace is hereby hiked to eight hundred dollars. In addition, you will be held until your trial on the weapons charge unless you can post bail of an additional five hundred. Do you have the money?"

"You know I don't, you old buzzard."

Rodgers smiled ever so sweetly. "We'll add an extra hundred dollars for contempt of court. Is there anything else you'd like to say?"

"Just that I hope you choke on your supper." Fargo couldn't resist baiting him.

"Make that an extra *two* hundred." The n. gistrate brought the gavel down with a resounding thump an ' bawled out, "Enough dillydallying. The next case, if you please!"

Brawny policemen escorted Fargo back to his cell. The only occupant was the snoring drunk in the bunk. Moving to the far side, where the reek was not as bad, Fargo hunkered and pondered. He'd had enough dealings with the law to know that San Francisco's finest would not take kindly to his accusation. If they were as corrupt as everyone claimed, they might see fit to arrange a little "accident." Maybe he would be shot while trying to escape. Or they might claim he hung himself out of grief or guilt.

So it was that when over an hour later Fargo heard plodding footsteps, he swung toward the door and coiled his legs, ready for anything.

Sergeant Harve Taylor shuffled into view. In his right hand he held a folded newspaper, which he shoved between the bars. "Here."

"What's that?" Fargo asked suspiciously.

"What the hell does it look like? It's a paper," the officer responded.

"I don't want it."

"You should." Taylor's thick lips quirked slyly upward and he spoke quietly so that only Fargo could hear. "It cost you

25

two hundred dollars." His big belly quaking, he let the newspaper drop and left.

"Bastard," Fargo said under his breath. He had no intention of picking it up, but after an hour had gone by he grew tired of twiddling his thumbs and gave in to temptation. It was well he did.

During his hearing before the magistrate, Fargo had been amazed at how much Judge Rodgers knew about him. He couldn't understand how, though. Not until he unfolded the *San Francisco Tribune* and saw the headline on the front page: RIOT AT DEN OF INIQUITY. The article went on to describe the fracas and gave a running account of the police response. Toward the end of the report was a paragraph that made the big man see red.

"Police have reason to believe that one of the men taken into custody was largely responsible for the destruction. Acting on information from an influential citizen, they have pinned the blame on one Skye Fargo, a buckskin-clad itinerant who allegedly threw the first punch."

Fargo nearly ripped the paper in half. He didn't need three guesses to know who the "influential citizen" had to be: none other than Bruno Scaglia. He would have given anything to get his hands on the man.

Disgusted, Fargo went to toss the paper aside and happened to glance at a smaller article on the same page. He went rigid as a tingle shot down his spine. "It can't be!" he blurted.

But it was. A reporter by the name of Carstairs had gone around talking to witnesses to the riot. Evidently he had been standing outside the casino when a man in buckskins was carried out. A "vivacious blonde," as Carstairs called her, had squealed, "Oh, Skye! What happened to you?" His nose for news perked, Carstairs had gone over and made the acquaintance of Miss Greta DuBois.

There in print was every word Fargo had told her about himself, along with her account of how he had tangled with certain "unsavory characters" she had never met before. To hear her tell it, the fight broke out when a roughneck made an insulting remark concerning her womanly virtue and Fargo had stepped in to defend her honor.

"Damn, damn, damn," Fargo grumbled. No wonder the judge had known everything! He would be lucky if he saw the light of day before next spring!

"Somethin' the matter, sonny?"

The man on the upper bunk had sat up. His hair hung in stringy wisps and his clothes were speckled with spots. Yawning, he scratched under an arm, then sniffed his fingers. "You sound a mite upset."

Fargo saw him start to slide down and snapped, "Stay right where you are, mister. My nose is about ready to fall off as it is."

"Oh?" The old-timer inhaled a few times, and cackled. "I reckon I do tend to get whiffy now and then. It's nothing a jump in the bay won't cure, though." Leaning back, he tilted his head and remarked, "I could be wrong. But you have the look of a man who wants to hit somebody."

"That would be just for starters," Fargo allowed. He checked the paper for more information on the riot. There was none. Tucked away on the society page, though, was a short story telling how a sterling pillar of the community, Mr. Bruno Scaglia, had donated a thousand dollars to the Police Benevolent Association. "Politics!" he declared.

The man on the bunk tittered. "Ain't it the truth! This old country of ours would be a heap better off if we could take all the politicians and the lawyers and ship the whole kit and caboodle to China. Let 'em drive the Celestials crazy!"

Fargo ignored the oldster in the hope the man would leave him alone. He should have known better.

"I heard a man say once that the only good lawyer is a dead lawyer," declared the font of wisdom, "and I believe it. Did you know that most politicians start out as lawyers and then get worse?" He scratched his chin and picked at his pants. "Why, when I was a sprout, people had more sense than to let those pesky varmints run things. We ought to pass a law that no one who uses fifty-cent words can run for public office. That would solve all our problems."

27

"If you say so," Fargo said, trying to show that he wasn't interested by his flat tone. Anyone else would have taken the hint. But not is fellow prisoner.

"Yes, indeedy. Once we started payin' 'em more than they need to put clothes on their backs and food on the table, we were done for. It's the money, you see. All they can think of is linin' their own pockets, no matter who they have to sell out. If you ask me, George Washington was the last honest politician we had. Did you hear how he fessed up to choppin' down that cherry tree? Now there was a man as honest as the day is long."

Fargo simply stared. As if he did not have enough problems, now he had to put up with the constant gum flapping of someone who was a few cards shy of a full deck.

"My ma wanted me to be a lawyer," the man revealed. "But I told her flat out that I could never go around cuttin' people up and takin' their innards out." Pausing, he plucked at his scruffy beard. "Wait a second. That was a sawbones she wanted me to be. How could I confuse the two?"

Resting his head on his forearms, Fargo closed his eyes and wondered what he had done to deserve all this.

"You ain't sick, are you, sonny?"

"No."

"That's a relief. I wouldn't want to catch anything off you. A man my age has to watch his health."

Just when Fargo thought things couldn't possibly get any worse, Sergeant Harve Taylor materialized and rapped on the bars with his key.

"On your feet, buckskin. This is your lucky day."

Two other policemen were waiting a few yards down the hall. Fargo saw that they both carried short clubs. "What are you up to?" he demanded.

"Someone is here to see you," Taylor said, opening the cell. "So hustle your butt out of there. It's in your best interests not to keep the man waiting."

Fargo knew of no one who would pay him a visit. "This hombre have a name?"

"William Hensley Nuttall."

"Never heard of him."

Taylor beckoned impatiently. "Neither have I, mister, but he must have clout somewhere because he spent five minutes with Judge Rodgers and got permission to talk to you. So, for the last time, get the hell up—or we'll drag you out."

Against Fargo's better judgment, he did as they wanted. Something told him that they were telling the truth. The sergeant assumed the lead and brought him to a spartan room containing a small table and two chairs. At the table sat a skinny man in a rumpled suit that clung loosely to his sparse frame. He had green eyes and a nose as big as an eagle's beak. On his head, framed by gray hair, rested a worn bowler.

But it wasn't the man who made Fargo's pulse speed up and his loins twitch. Standing on either side of the room were two incredibly beautiful women, one a redhead, the other sporting a luxurious main of black hair that cascaded well past her shoulders. Both had green eyes, high cheekbones, and lips like ripe strawberries. Both wore plain but tight dresses that accented their equally ripe bodies.

"That will be all, Sergeant," the man said in a surprisingly deep voice. "We'll call you when we're ready."

Taylor could not take his eyes off the women. "Are you sure, Mr. Nuttall, sir?" he responded. "I don't mind staying. This guy might cause trouble."

"You heard me. Now run along." Nuttall dismissed the officer with a wave of his hand.

Reluctantly, Harve Taylor departed. No sooner did the door close than the black-haired beauty vented an unladylike snort and declared, "What a pig! For two cents I'd cut him into little pieces and feed him to the sharks."

Fargo smiled at her. Here was a woman who took no guff from any man. A woman who reacted to his smile with another snort and a toss of her mane.

"Men!"

William Hensley Nuttall cleared his throat. "Not now, Melissa. Restrain that temper of yours while I conduct the interview." Arching his eyebrows at Fargo, he added, "You'll have to forgive my daughter. She has always been the hothead

29

of the family. You would think it would be the other way around, since Davina has the red hair."

"Father, please," Melissa said. "We don't even know this man."

Now that they mentioned it, Fargo could see a certain resemblance in their features. The redhead took the antics of the other two in stride, as if she were used to their squabbling.

Nodding at the other chair, Nuttall introduced himself and said, "Why don't you have a seat, Mr. Fargo. We have a lot to discuss."

The big man accepted the offer. Melissa and Davina studied him as they might something under a microscope, Melissa with a frown, Davina with no hint of emotion. "You can start by telling me what this is all about."

"Very well. I read in the newspaper that you are a scout with vast experience. It mentioned that you have even been to Washington Territory."

"A few times," Fargo confirmed.

"Most excellent!" Nuttall said, rubbing his hands in excitement. "Then you are just the man we are looking for. I want to hire you to guide our expedition into a remote range seldom visited by white men."

"Let me guess. You're after gold or silver."

Father and daughters laughed. "Goodness gracious, no!" Nuttall declared. "I want to go there to paint birds."

3

Skye Fargo almost groaned out loud. The last time he had been to San Francisco he had hooked up with a loco professor who had hired him to help transport a bunch of bones and animal hides east to the States. They had been fortunate to get there in one piece. "You're not from one of those places like Harvard or Yale, are you?"

"My paintings grace the corridors of a few institutions of higher learning, but I'm not connected with any one school," Nuttall responded. "Why do you ask?"

"Never mind. Go on."

Nuttall leaned down to the left and produced a large but thin leather carrying case that had been propped against his chair. "I don't suppose you are familiar with my work?"

"Can't say as I am," Fargo admitted.

Melissa indulged in her snort. "How typical of these rustic types, Father. They have no sense of culture. If this clod knew how famous you are—"

"Enough," Nuttall chided while unzipping the case. "I will not have you antagonizing Mr. Fargo when we need his services so badly."

"We could manage without him," Melissa countered sullenly. "After all, how hard can it be to find a *mountain*?"

The painter sighed. "We have been through this so many times, my dear, that I should have thought you would know better by now," he said with the air of someone whose patience was being sorely tested. "It is my policy to never, ever go on an expedition into an unmapped area without a reliable guide. It is simply too dangerous. Only a complete idiot would do otherwise." He glanced across the table. "Wouldn't you agree, sir?"

"Yes," Fargo said, his estimation of the easterner rising a notch. Too many tenderfeet had the mistaken notion that they could handle anything the wilderness threw at them. As a result, the wagon trails across the plains and mountains were littered with the bones of those who had learned the hard way that a person had to know his limitations.

"Here," Nuttall said, swinging the case around so that its contents were in plain view. "Take a look at these. They will show you far better than words why I need your help."

Seven marvelous paintings were spread out for Fargo to examine. They all depicted birds and were remarkable for their vivid detail. One was a bald eagle shown in flight, another a sage hen scratching in the dust. Each was so realistic that Fargo had the impression he was peering through a window at an actual creature. "You do nice work," he said, and was treated to yet another of Melissa's snorts.

"Nice work? You dolt! My father is the premier wildlife painter of our generation. His work graces the White House and the homes of a dozen senators. His fame is so great that the Queen of England commissioned a piece." Smirking, she taunted, "Now what do you think?"

Fargo had taken all the abuse from her he was going to abide. Locking his eyes on hers, he said, "I think you're a fine-looking woman, but that mouth of yours must get you in a heap of trouble. Maybe it's time you grew up and learned to control your tongue."

Melissa Nuttall turned scarlet, then sputtered as if she were having a fit. Davina rocked with hearty laughter. Their father did a double take, then lowered his head to hide his wide grin as his shoulders silently quaked.

"How dare you insult me!" the raven-haired firebrand snapped, taking a step and balling a fist. "I can't think of one good reason why I shouldn't box your ears!"

"I can," Fargo said casually. "I'd slap you so hard that your own ears would ring."

"But I'm a woman!"

"So what? No one has the right to put a hand on anyone else. If they do, they have to suffer the consequences."

Simmering, Melissa stalked toward the door. "This is hopeless, Father. The man is a barbarian, a Goth in frontier garb. Let's find someone who has proper manners."

William Nuttall jabbed a finger at her. "Enough! You will be still and be quiet! I can't conduct business with you interrupting every three seconds." Taking a breath to calm himself, he went on. "Mr. Fargo strikes me as being perfect for the job. You're just upset because you've finally met a man with enough fortitude to stand up to you."

Fargo ignored the withering stare Melissa gave him and rested his elbows on the edge of the table. "Tell me more about this job, mister. Where exactly do you want to go? What are you after?"

From under the paintings Nuttall slid a folded sheet which he spread out to reveal a recent map of Washington Territory. Since the region was largely unexplored, except for several rivers that had been navigated by missionaries and trappers, much of the interior was blank. A few mountain ranges were marked, and the artist tapped a slender finger on one of them in the south-central part of the territory, not all that far north of the Columbia River, as the crow flies.

"Are you familiar with this area?" the artist inquired.

"Familiar enough to know that only one or two white men have ever gone there," Fargo remarked. "The Indians aren't very friendly. A few years back Jed Smith took his trapping brigade in and they were massacred by the Umpquas. Smith was lucky to get out with his hide intact."

If the news had any effect, Nuttall did not show it. "What about Mount Saint Helens? Do you think you could find your way there?"

A chill rippled down Fargo's spine. He wasn't one for premonitions and such, but he had heard enough about that particular mountain to fill him with a sense of foreboding. "I could, yes. But you should think twice if that's where you're fixing to go. The Indians stay shy of it. They say it's bad medicine, that anyone who goes there will die."

33

"Bad medicine?" Melissa tittered. "Do you really expect us to put any credence in a silly superstition?"

"I would, if I were you," Fargo said. "The Indians have been in this country a far sight longer than we have. Take the Klikitat, for instance. They've lived in that exact area for more years than anyone can count. I ran into a few of them at Fort Vancouver once. They were there trading furs."

"So?" Melissa said.

"So they told me that no one in their tribe goes anywhere near Mount Saint Helens. It's taboo, you might say."

Nuttall was extremely interested. "Did they happen to tell you why?"

Fargo nodded. "The Klikitat believe a race of hairy giants live there. The Skoo-kum, these giants are called, and they're real fond of human flesh. They're over eight feet tall, weigh hundreds of pounds, leave footprints over a foot and a half long, and stink to high heaven." he would have gone on, but Melissa's laughter drowned him out.

"Skoo-kum!" she exclaimed. "Oh, please! Now I've heard everything! We're not about to let such drivel stop us."

The painter leaned toward Fargo. "Pay her no mind. And tell me. These Klikitat you mentioned. They sound friendly enough, so couldn't we hire a few of them to guide us?"

"Not if we want to go on breathing," Fargo said. "Sure, the three warriors at the fort were on their best behavior because they wanted to get their hands on some trade goods. But if we were caught in their territory, we'd end up like Jed Smith's men."

The painter glanced at the map and touched a fingertip to Mount Saint Helens. "Despite the dangers, Mr. Fargo, I am bound and determined to go there."

"What's so damned important that you'd risk getting your throat slit?"

A dreamy look came over the man. "Ever since I was a small boy, I've had a passion for two things in life: birds and painting. At the age of eleven, when most boys my age were out shooting squirrels or fishing or playing in swimming holes, I was sketching every bird I could find. I drew them all, from the smallest finch to the biggest owls." Nuttall paused and actually caressed the painting he had done of the eagle as if it were a woman's thigh. "But I tired of doing the same birds all the time. I needed to find new ones to whet my interest. So after Princeton I traveled far and wide. In Florida I painted storks and herons. In the Rockies I painted eagles and hawks. I've done them all, from one coast to the other."

Fargo was afraid the artist would go into a long-winded account of every bird he had ever done, so he prompted, "That's all well and good. But what does it have to do with Mount Saint Helens?"

"There came a time when I had done every bird known. In order to carry on with my life's work, I began seeking out unknown types, birds only rumored to exist. In the past year alone I've done a rare hummingbird and an even rarer copper-tailed trogon. Now I'm after a blue tanager."

"I've never seen one."

"No one has, Mr. Fargo. Western tanagers have bright red heads and yellow bodies, as I'm sure you're aware. But a few years ago a traveler named Kane passed along the Washington coast and heard about a blue tanager rumored to live on and around Mount Saint Helens."

Fargo sat back, careful to conceal his feelings. The truth was that although he liked Nuttall and admired the artist's talent, the man was letting his obsession with birds get him in over his head. The Skoo-kum aside, a journey to Mount Saint Helens would be downright grueling. They would have to contend with hostile Indians, with grizzlies and mountain lions and other beasts. And as if that were not enough, Mount Saint Helens was a *volcano*. Smoke spewed from it every now and then, and there were some who claimed that one day it was going to blow its top in an eruption that would put old-time Vesuvius to shame. He didn't care to be in its vicinity when that happened.

A thought struck him, prompting Fargo to ask, "What about your daughters? Are you planning to take them along?"

Melissa answered first. "I'd like to see him try to stop us! Where our father goes, we go. Right, sis?"

Davina, who had not uttered a single word during the whole talk, merely nodded.

"Ever since they were old enough to walk, I've taken them on my little expeditions," Nuttall explained. "They go with me everywhere."

"This time you might be biting off more than you can chew," Fargo warned.

Nuttall frowned. "I'm not an imbecile, Mr. Fargo. I've done my research. I know that two years ago the Yakima Indians led an uprising in that region, but they were forced to give in and sign a treaty. Since then all the tribes have been at peace, although no one knows how long that will last." Beginning to gather his paintings, he said, "I don't think there is any better time than right now for me to go after the blue tanager. To that end, I have arranged with Judge Rodgers to have the charges against you dropped and to pay all your fines if you agree to serve as our guide. In addition, I will pay you whatever is fair for your services."

It was a hell of a choice, Fargo mused. Either he rotted behind bars until the magistrate saw fit to let him out, or he acted as nursemaid for three people just asking to get themselves and everyone with them chopped into tiny pieces.

"I'm afraid I must have your decision before I leave this room," Nuttall said. "And there is something you should know that might help you make the right choice."

"I can hardly wait to hear it."

"Rodgers told me that the owner of the gambling hall has hired an attorney with the intent of suing you for the damages."

"I know. He mentioned it. But it won't do any good. I don't have any money left."

"The judge hinted that he might make you work off what you owe. A thousand dollars, I think he said." Nuttall reflected a moment. "At two dollars a day, it shouldn't take you more than a year and a half."

There was no way in hell Fargo was going to let himself be roped into tending bar or mopping floors for months on end when someone else was to blame for the riot. He was between the proverbial rock and a hard place. Damned if he did, twice damned if he didn't. "Hell," he grumbled, "I reckon you've hired yourself a guide."

William Hensley Nuttall beamed. "I'm delighted to have you on board, so to speak."

"Speak for yourself," Melissa interjected.

The painter rolled his eyes, then continued. "Give me half an hour to settle accounts with Judge Rodgers and arrange for your release. Afterward we'll go over the plans I've come up with and you can point out any mistakes I've made."

True to the artist's word, within thirty minutes of being returned to his cell, Fargo stood on the front steps of the precinct house, his Colt and his Arkansas toothpick in a small sack in his left hand, a free man. None other than Sergeant Taylor had closed the door behind him, and it had taken all of Fargo's self-control to keep from planting his fist in the smirking policeman's face. He knew Taylor had stolen his money, and knew that the sergeant knew he knew. It was all the harder to bear because Taylor was also aware there was nothing he could do about it without proof.

The Nuttall clan awaited him. A black hansom cab carried them to a luxury hotel, where Fargo was given a plush room adjoining their suite. Neither of the women uttered a word the whole time. Their father, predictably, went on and on about birds.

Fargo had to concede that for all his faults, William Nuttall was a thorough man. The artist had the expedition laid out with military precision. He had already chartered a small clipper ship to transport them and their belongings up the coast of California and on to the mouth of the mighty Columbia River. There, they would turn inland to a point due south of Mount Saint Helens and be deposited on shore. From the river to the volcano was a distance of forty-two miles, over some of the most rugged terrain in the world.

Despite that drawback, the route picked was the quickest, straightest course. Their only other choices were to sail clean up to Aberdeen and then strike overland one hundred miles, which would take three times as long, or to sail all the way up and around the Olympic Peninsula and then down Puget Sound to Olympia and on to Mount Saint Helens, which would entail even more time.

Fargo praised the painter for his decision and was amazed when the man blushed. Since it had been his experience that most easterners had a habit of toting more supplies than were needed on long treks, he thought to ask, "What are you bringing along?"

Nuttall handed over a list of every item. Once more Fargo was impressed. From tents to a portable oven, everything was essential. Nuttall had even arranged passage for six horses. "You weren't lying when you claimed that you've done this before."

"As you can see, we're all set," the artist replied. "Our ship sails tomorrow at noon. Will that give you enough time to get whatever you want to take?"

"A couple of boxes of ammo are all I need," Fargo said. "But I'd like to take my own horse, if you don't mind. Will that be a problem?"

"None at all. The captain has a special hold for livestock. I'll contact him first thing in the morning."

Outside, the sun was going down. To the west the sea blazed with brilliant hues of red, orange, and yellow. Fargo glanced out the window, donned his hat, and rose. "Then I'll see you at the crack of dawn."

Nuttall also stood. "You're going out?" he asked with a trace of unease.

"There's some unfinished business I have to tend to," Fargo explained. Opening the sack, he removed the toothpick and slid the slim knife into the sheath attached to his right ankle. The Colt went under his shirt, as before. When he straightened, he found all three of his benefactors watching him closely.

"You're not thinking of running out on us, are you, big man?" Melissa asked bluntly. "Because if you are, we'll see to it that Judge Rodgers issues a warrant for your arrest, and you'll find yourself back in jail so fast it will make your head spin."

Fargo had seldom met a woman so contrary. He didn't even look at her as he made for the door. "I gave you my word, didn't I?"

"Let me guess," Melissa cracked. "You want us to believe that you're one of those men whose word is his bond, who does as he says he will no matter what?" She chortled as if the very idea were hilarious.

His hand on the smooth doorknob, Fargo paused. "Frankly, lady, I don't give a damn what you believe. Just count on me being here when the sun comes up." Nodding at her father and the redhead, Fargo went out and down the carpeted stairs to the spacious lobby.

Since the painter had given Fargo a fifty-dollar advance on his wages, he went straight to the row of hansoms waiting at the corner and held five dollars out to the grizzled driver of the first cab.

The man stared at the money as if it were counterfeit. "What's this for?"

"It's how much extra you'll get if you can track down the man I'm looking for," Fargo said.

"I take it by your tone that he ain't exactly your best friend. Who might this gentleman be?"

"Bruno Scaglia."

Astonishment etched the driver's face. "Are you sure that you know what you're doing, mister? No one in their right mind wants to tangle with that he-snake."

"Can you find him?"

"I might be able to," the driver said hesitantly. "I've lived in this city since I came out to Californy about ten years ago, so I know it like I do the back of my hand. I can recognize most of the bigwigs on sight. And I know where most of them like to spend their time."

Fargo placed the money in the man's hand and went to climb into the two-wheeled carriage. "Then let's get going."

"Not so fast," the driver said. "All the money in the world won't keep me out of a pine box if you cause trouble for that bastard and later he finds out I was the one who took you to see him."

"He'll never know," Fargo said. As added incentive he forked over another five.

Greed and conscience waged a brief battle and greed won. The driver scampered up into the elevated seat at the rear of the carriage, waited for Fargo to settle in, and cracked his whip. The cab lurched, then clattered along smoothly while gaining speed.

The brisk breeze off the bay invigorated Fargo. Soon the hansom cab reached a series of low hills. From the crown of each he glimpsed a number of high-masted ships down in the harbor, and he wondered which was the one he would be sailing on with the next tide.

They left the business district and the seedier part of the city behind and entered a neighborhood where all the homes were as huge as palaces. Most boasted neatly tended lawns and were bordered by high fences. These were the estates of the city's well-to-do.

At the next corner the driver turned right. Fargo noticed a wrought iron gate bearing a gold-embossed sign that read THE NOB HILL COUNTRY CLUB. The cab slowed. When they came to the end of the block, the driver again wheeled to the right and pulled under a tree at the side of the narrow street.

"This is it, mister."

Fargo climbed out. Except for a small carriage hundreds of yards away, they were the only traffic. "Here?" he said, gauging the height of the wall at eight feet.

"Scaglia is a member. He likes to think of himself as one of the city's upper crust now that he has money, but the society types don't want anything to do with him." The driver removed his top hat to mop his bald pate with a handkerchief. "The word is that he likes to eat his supper at the club about five nights a week. I've brought him here twice myself in the past year. If you aim to brace him, this is the best place to do it."

Fargo wasn't so certain. For one thing, he would stand out like a sore thumb if caught on the grounds, since it was highly unlikely any of the members were in the habit of wearing buckskins. For another, there would be too many people around. He needed privacy. "There has to be somewhere else."

"If you want to try trailing him all over creation," the driver said. "Scaglia owns about six resorts and has his hooks into another twenty more. There's no telling which one he'll go to after he's done eating. And if he spots us, we're finished."

Slipping a hand into his pocket for his money, Fargo turned. "If anyone asks, you've never met me. I never took your cab."

"Do I look that stupid?" the man responded. "Hell, from this minute on I don't know you from Adam." Accepting his fare, he hustled off and never glanced back.

Fargo wasted no time. A low limb enabled him to climb into the tree. Working his way from branch to branch, he balanced on a thick one that extended over the top of the wall. By shimmying outward, he eventually reached a spot above a narrow path that paralleled it. The branch bent but didn't break. Firming his grip, he swung off and dropped lightly to the soft soil below.

Before Fargo could decide which direction to go, an ominous growl issued from the base of the trees that grew in that corner of the grounds. He whirled as a flowing dark shape detached itself from the shadows and padded toward him.

It was a huge dog.

4

The dog never slowed. It never barked. It simply lowered its head, bared its tapered fangs, and attacked in a swift rush.

Skye Fargo barely had time to throw his arms up to protect his throat. The beast sprang, its jaws clamping onto his left forearm even as it barreled into his chest with the force of a battering ram and knocked him back against the wall. Snarling and snapping, it reared on its hind legs and tried to get at his face.

Fargo had never seen its like before. The brute was dark gray, its shoulders as high as his waist. Bulky with rippling sinews, it weighed close to two hundred pounds. Fighting it was like battling a small bear. He connected with a blow to the head, but all that did was send the animal into a frenzy.

Those enormous jaws swept at Fargo's neck. He thrust outward, clamping both hands on the dog's throat. It took all his strength to hold the creature at bay. Slavering and growling, the dog edged closer, ever closer. Fargo drove his knee into the beast's middle, eliciting a yelp, then shoved and darted to the right to gain room to maneuver.

The dog was on him in a twinkling. Fargo yanked his hand back or he would have lost it. Retreating rapidly, he cast about for a weapon, since he didn't dare use his gun. The shot would alert the club staff, and Scaglia.

Lying beside the trail was a short length of broken branch. Fargo scooped it up and braced himself just as the animal launched itself into the air. His swing was perfect. The branch caught the dog on the side of the head—and broke into small

42

bits. The wood was dead, as useless as a wad of paper. He threw the rest aside.

Now the dog was on all fours, crouched low with its hackles raised. Head tilted, its dark eyes slits of bestial hatred, it inched forward.

Off through the trees, perhaps a hundred yards or so, stood the ornate country club. For all Fargo knew, members were out strolling the grounds, getting some exercise. He had to take care of the dog before someone heard it and investigated.

Suddenly the animal charged. It aimed low this time, chomping at Fargo's thigh. The big man twisted, sparing his leg, but as he did his foot snagged on a clump of weeds. He stumbled. The dog was on him before he could right himself. They both went down, Fargo on his back, the brute astride him and trying to rip open the soft flesh at the base of his throat.

Again Fargo strained to hold the slavering canine off. Warm drops of saliva splattered his face. Claws raked his torso and legs.

Tensing, Fargo hurled the dog to the right. It slipped but promptly scrambled erect and came at him like a living bolt of lightning. Fargo's hand swooped to his right boot. The Arkansas toothpick streaked clear. He had it only as high as his knees when the dog reached him, but that proved to be high enough.

The beast's own momentum impaled it on the blade. Yipping once, it scampered to the left and paused, breathing heavily while blood oozed from a hole in its chest.

Fargo stared at the thin knife in his hand. He hadn't wanted to kill the dog, but it had left him no choice. It weakened quickly, sagging onto its belly and lying there with pink foam ringing its mouth. When it keeled onto its side and quivered, Fargo made bold, grabbing it by the front paws and dragging the body under cover of the lengthening shadows.

The sun was almost gone. Twilight claimed the city by the bay, and a few stars twinkled to the north.

Fargo wiped the blade clean on the grass and replaced it. Hastening along the trail, he came to a junction. Trimmed hedges formed part of a verdant garden rife with flowers of every size and color. Ducking low, Fargo glided along the hedge to an adjoining footpath that led to a side door in the building. Rather than enter, he crawled behind a row of short shrubs and waited for darkness to fully descend.

Hardly was Fargo in place than the door opened and three well-dressed men emerged. One lit a fat cigar as they strolled off. They were talking so low that it was hard for Fargo to make out what they were saying, but it had something to do with investing in a local business.

As night spread, lights came on. Several more members came out for a breath of fresh air. Fargo hoped that Scaglia would be among them, but he had no such luck.

The clatter of carriages and cabs in front of the club told Fargo that the supper crowd was arriving. Rising, he crept the length of the building to the rear corner, peering in every window he passed. In one lavish room he saw men seated on sofas and divans, reading. In another were a half dozen of San Francisco's wealthiest, playing friendly games of billiards. In yet a third, a woman built like a bull buffalo was giving an elderly gentleman a massage.

The back door had a sign over it that read SERVANTS' ENTRANCE. Fargo checked all around him before easing the door inward and peeking inside. A long, murky hall connected to a kitchen. Through another doorway at the far end a large stove and a table laden with bowls and pans were visible. Voices could be heard. From the hustle and bustle, he guessed the cooks were hard at work.

Off the hall were three closed doors, as well. Quickly entering, Fargo dashed to the nearest. He had stumbled on a wide closet filled with supplies. From racks on the left wall hung various kitchen clothes.

Closing the door behind him, Fargo pulled a pair of baggy white pants on over his own. An equally loose-fitting white shirt completed his disguise. Under it he shoved his hat. It gave him a paunch the size of a keg of ale.

Warily stepping out, Fargo slowly approached the kitchen. Two men and two women were busily preparing all kinds of meals. The pace was so hectic that they were constantly in motion, either stirring or ladling or carving. Through a swinging door on the opposite side filed one waiter after another, either to bark out an order or to pick up a tray laden with plates and bowls of food.

There was another door midway along the left-hand wall. Taking a brazen gamble, Fargo picked up a high pile of folded white napkins that were on a small table close by, hoisted them to his shoulder to hide his face, and strode toward that door as if he had every right to be there and knew just what he was doing. One of the cooks glanced at him and then resumed slicing a juicy roast into thin strips.

Once through the door, Fargo held onto the napkins, just in case. A narrow hall brought him to a wider one. Staying well back in the shadows, he mulled over whether to keep going or to turn back. Finding Scaglia in a building that size would take some doing, and there was every chance he would be discovered before he did. He chided himself for not thinking the whole thing through ahead of time.

Fargo began to swing around just as low voices sounded. A moment later, four men appeared and climbed a flight of spiral stairs. In their lead, sauntering along as if he owned the place, was none other than Bruno Scaglia.

The hunted had blundered upon the hunter.

Staying put until they had climbed from sight, Fargo made sure to keep the pile of napkins close to his head, then followed. Cigar smoke hung heavy in the air, its acrid scent mixed with that of the lemon polish used on the walls and banister.

A beanpole of a man, in a suit that must have cost more than most people earned in six months, came down the stairs toward Fargo. He immediately hunched his shoulders and stooped to disguise his size. Fargo also made a point of looking at the wall, but watched the man on the sly out of the corner of one eye.

The Trailsman need not have worried. The member paid no attention to him at all. It was as if he were invisible. Nose in the air, humming to himself, the man went on down. Evidently club patrons considered the hired staff beneath their notice.

Encouraged, Fargo stopped on the landing. Scaglia and those with him were halfway down a wide corridor graced by works of art and covered with carpet inches thick. They halted at a door. The kingpin said a few words that made the others laugh. After pumping his hand, the trio walked on while Scaglia passed through the doorway.

Fargo hustled to within a stride of the room and paused to listen. From within came a rustling sound and a drawn-out sigh. Since no one else was in the corridor, Fargo slipped in and quietly shut the door behind him.

It was a reading room. Three of the walls were lined with crammed bookshelves, the fourth contained a large window framed by gold curtains. Several high-backed chairs and a small circular table on which rested five or six newspapers were the only furniture.

Bruno Scaglia sat in the chair nearest the window, a paper in his lap, in the act of lighting a cigarette. He looked absently around at the click of the door, and his bushy eyebrows arched. "Don't you have the wrong place, boy?" he asked, sneering. "The dining room is on the first floor." Chortling at his humor, he puffed a few times and started to slide his silver cigarette case into a jacket pocket. Only then did he notice that Fargo was still there.

"What's the matter, stupid? Didn't you hear me?"

Standing so Scaglia could see his profile but not his full face, Fargo deposited the napkins on a chair.

"If you don't get the hell out of here, I'll have you fired," Scaglia stated. "If you don't believe I can, just ask around. No one gives me trouble. Ever."

"But you sure cause a lot of trouble, don't you?" Fargo said as he pivoted.

"*You!*" Scaglia heaved his enormous form out of the chair. Surprisingly, he showed no fear or concern. In fact, he laughed and said, "You must think that you're mighty clever, sneaking in here the way you've done. But between you and me, it's the dumbest stunt you've ever pulled."

"I want you to leave Greta DuBois alone," Fargo said.

Scaglia let the paper drop and made a tepee of his thick fingers. "So that's what this is all about. That stinking whore. Well, never let it be said that I'm not a reasonable man. If you want me to stay away from her, then that's exactly what I'll do."

Fargo knew it was a ruse of some kind. "Why is it that I don't believe you?"

The kingpin snickered. "Maybe I've misjudged you. Maybe you're not as brainless as I thought." Lowering his arms, he said with a perverse glee, "No one will ever lay a finger on your girlfriend again, mister. Not unless they know exactly where to dig to find her bones."

"What?"

"You heard me. No one treats me the way she did. Last night I was waiting in her apartment when she came home. She cried and begged, like they always do, but I still stabbed her twenty or thirty times. I can't remember exactly how many. I was so mad that once I started, I couldn't stop." Scaglia shrugged. "After I had my way with her, of course."

A crimson haze seemed to fill the room. Fargo was in motion before he quite realized what he was doing. At a full run he plowed into the bigger man just as Scaglia straightened, sending them both crashing into the wall. In his blind fury he lashed out, landing a punch to the jaw that had no effect. Scaglia had braced himself in time, and his answering blow sent Fargo flying into the chair in front of them. The chair went down, Fargo with it.

Pushing onto his hands and knees, Fargo barely saw the foot that hooked into his ribs and lifted him clean off the floor. He bounced off a bookcase, striking it so hard that books rained down on him when he hit the floor. Leaping up, he was puzzled to see his enemy just standing there.

Scaglia stooped close to the overturned chair, and when he rose he held his cane. "Remember this?" he asked, giving it a twist. The four-inch blade popped out. "If you don't, allow me to refresh your memory." Bellowing, he closed in, swinging the cane with lethal skill.

In the gambling hall the previous night Fargo had been hemmed in by the crowd. In the reading room he had more space, but not much more. The chairs and the table blocked him in as he danced to the right. The cane whisked past his shoulder, near enough to nick the white shirt. He vaulted into the clear, landing beyond the table and spinning to keep from being stabbed in the back.

"Hop like a jackrabbit all you want," Scaglia said. "It won't help you none." The cane lanced through the air.

Fargo ducked, felt the steel brush his hair, and dodged to the left. The cane gave the kingpin an added three-foot reach, which Scaglia took full advantage of. Again and again Fargo had to evade the gleaming tip. Once it tore his pants. Another stab nearly put a new hole in his ear.

Every time Fargo tired to slip past the blade to get at Scaglia, he was thwarted. Circling, he came to a chair and put it between them. Scaglia speared the cane over the top and to either side but missed. Fargo attempted to grab it, without success.

Suddenly Scaglia stopped. "It's too bad my boys are waiting out front, or you wouldn't still be standing." Somewhere on the floor a voice called out, and he laughed. "Hear that, mister? Others will be here soon. I'll have them turn you over to the police. Then, just for the hell of it, I'm going to see that you get the blame for your girlfriend's murder. Can you think of anything more fitting?"

Fargo was growing desperate. Grabbing the back of the chair, he pushed, shoving it forward. Scaglia was caught flat-footed. The chair crashed into him and he staggered. Taking a flying dive, Fargo tackled Scaglia and they thudded onto their sides. Instantly Scaglia arced the cane on high to thrust it, but his arm struck the table.

Fargo planted his knuckles on the man's mouth. The punch rocked Scaglia, dazing him long enough for Fargo to rise onto his knees and grab the cane with both hands. With a brutal wrench, Fargo tore the weapon free. As he went to rise, Scaglia grasped his ankle and heaved. He was flipped into a chair and wound up on the floor again, his legs pinned under it. Somehow, he lost the cane.

Above him loomed Bruno Scaglia. Seized by blood lust, the

kingpin pounced, his huge fingers bent like talons. Fargo jerked to one side but Scaglia was amazingly quick for one so enormous. The next moment those fingers were squeezing like a vise around Fargo's throat.

Bucking like a mustang, Fargo sought to break loose. But Scaglia was leaning on the chair, trapping him in place. He couldn't get enough leverage. Bit by bit the life was being choked from his body and there wasn't a thing he could do. He rained blows, but he might as well have been hitting solid granite. Throwing his entire weight to the right proved just as fruitless.

As Fargo groped the floor for purchase, his fingers closed on a smooth, slender object. He did not need to look at it to know what it was. Raising it, he sheared the blade into Scaglia's neck just under the jaw. The terror of the Barbary Coast shrieked like a mountain lion and hurtled up off the chair. A red geyser streamed in his wake.

Flinging the chair off himself, Fargo jumped up. Scaglia was tottering toward the door, a dead man, even if he wouldn't admit it yet. Out in the hall, footsteps pounded. There were harsh yells.

Fargo had no way out. Or did he? Hefting the table, he turned to the window and threw it. Glass shattered in tiny shards, tinkling over the floor. In a bound Fargo was at the sill. Two floors below grew shrubbery.

A glance back showed Scaglia on his knees, doubled over at the base of the door. Someone was on the other side, pushing to get in, but the heavy body prevented the door from opening.

Swiftly Fargo stripped off the white shirt and pants. Shoving his hat onto his head, he climbed on the sill, poised with a hand on either jamb, then vaulted into space. The shrubs proved a lot harder than they looked, their tiny branches scratching at his face and arms. But they did as he intended and broke his fall. Lurching into the open, he glimpsed faces peering at him from several windows and ran into the garden.

A pistol cracked. Then another. Lead thudded into the ground on both sides of Fargo. He zigzagged, but he was still quite a distance from cover and the shooters were bound to get him at that range.

Then a strange thing happened. From behind the hedge to the west another gun boomed. This shooter, though, fired at the club instead of at Fargo. He heard glass break, and startled oaths. A lithe figure appeared, motioning for him to hurry. Bewildered, he did. Unexpectedly another dog materialized out of empty air and bore down on him. He whirled to meet it but the beast never reached him.

The figure near the hedge fired twice. Each slug scored. The dog crumpled in midstride and rolled to a stop almost at Fargo's feet. A pair of neat holes above the eyes testified to the shooter's accuracy.

Shots from the building peppered the soil as Fargo sprinted the remaining yards. His guardian angel covered him every step of the way. Stopping once he'd rounded the hedge, Fargo was shocked to see who had come to his rescue. Even though her features were clouded by shadow and she had on pants and a shirt instead of a dress, there was no mistaking the rich red hair that framed her lovely face. "Davina?"

"Go!" she urged, giving him a push. "They'll be on us in a minute. I'll be right behind you."

Those were the first words she has spoken to him, and until then Fargo had no idea her voice was as sultry as a hot summer's day and as throaty as the purr of a contented cat. He headed for the wall as bullets tore through the hedge around them. She was true to her word, never slackening even when he ran at his top speed. She was, to put it mildly, a bundle of surprises. And there were more to come.

At the wall Davina slid the pistol into a holster under her lightweight jacket, cupped her hands, and said, "Here. You first. I'll give you a boost."

"I can manage on my own, thanks," Fargo responded. The top was only two feet above his head. Raising his arms, he coiled to jump, when from the garden came the sounds of pursuit.

"Don't be pigheaded, damn it," Davina snapped. "I gave you more credit than that."

Growing more confused by the second, Fargo did as she requested. She was much stronger than she seemed; he nearly overshot the top. Crouching, he lowered his arm and said, "Grab hold!"

Davina shook her head while backing up. She took a breath, then exploded into motion. Darting toward him, she vaulted upward at just the right moment. Her hands gripped the edge and she swung up unaided, alighting with all the grace of a sleek panther. "What are you waiting for?" she asked.

Fargo dropped outside the grounds. He was taken aback to find a hansom cab waiting for them. The redhead reached it first and gave the driver directions. As Fargo began to climb in beside her, the man cracked his whip and the horse took off as if its tail were ablaze. Fargo was pitched against her. For a few delightful seconds his face was nestled in a heavenly soft bosom and he inhaled the heady scent of lavender. Davina shoved him off just as they rounded a corner on one wheel, which threw her against him. They were face to face, nose to nose, her rosy lips nearly brushing his. He smiled, but she betrayed no emotion at all and scooted back to her side.

"What was that all about back there? I never took you for the country club type."

They were traveling at a reckless rate. Fargo shifted to gaze out the rear window but saw no sign of anyone after them. "I balanced the scales," he said.

"What scales?" Davina probed, and when he wouldn't answer, she queried, "What kind of trouble did you get into this time?"

Fargo sank back and confirmed he still had his Colt. "I'm the one who should be asking the questions, lady," he responded. "What the blazes were you doing there? And don't try to tell me you were out picking flowers."

A grin tugged at her full mouth. "I trailed you from the hotel, then hung around to see what would happen."

"I didn't think you cared that much," Fargo quipped.

"I did it for my father. He has his heart set on painting a blue tanager, and my sister and I will do whatever it takes to make his dream come true. Including making sure that you show up at the pier on time." Davina smoothed her jacket, unconsciously enhancing the swell of her breasts. "And since you're no doubt curious, I learned to shoot when I was ten. I've always been a bit of a tomboy."

"You won't hear me complain."

"What I'd like to hear, Mr. Fargo, is your promise that you won't go gallivanting off again before we sail tomorrow," Davina said.

"You'd take me at my word?" Fargo wondered, remembering Melissa's lack of faith.

"Unlike my sister, I know an honest man when I meet one. We're very different, she and I. Never make the mistake of assuming we think alike."

It gave Fargo much to reflect on during the ride back to the hotel. Long afterward, he lay on his back in his bed, relishing the memory of the brief contact their bodies had made. Now there was a woman after his own heart! As tough as tempered steel, yet as soft as satin.

Maybe, just maybe, the trek to Mount Saint Helens would turn out to be a lot more interesting than he had figured.

5

The expedition got off to a fine start. Or so Fargo thought at the time.

As soon as the golden sun cleared the hazy horizon he had gone to the livery on Fremont Street and paid his bill. The Ovaro pranced and nuzzled him in its eagerness to get out of the cramped stall. In that respect the pinto stallion was a lot like Fargo himself. Neither could stand to be cooped up for any length of time.

The Nuttalls were about to climb the gangplank when Fargo rode up. He was introduced to the captain, a crusty old salt named Gibson. Crewmen were called to lead the Ovaro onto the ship, but Fargo insisted on handling the chore himself. He had reservations about whether the stallion would take to sea travel, but his doubts vanished once he saw the hold in which the animals were kept. There was ample hay and oats and plenty of room for the horses to stretch their legs.

William Nuttall's equipment and supplies were loaded. Last-minute additions were also hustled aboard, mainly cargo the *Celeste* would take on to Olympia and other points north after dropping off the painter's party. And then, mere minutes before the vessel was set to sail and just as the crew was about to raise the gangplank, three men in overalls, wool shirts, and round caps showed up.

Fargo was on the bow, observing the whirl of activity. He saw the newcomers talking to Captain Gibson. A man in a blue cap pulled an envelope from a pocket and handed it over. Gibson inspected the contents, gave a curt nod, and ushered them below deck.

At noon the clipper ship got underway. The captain barked commands as only a seasoned sea wolf could. In no time the anchor was raised, the sails were unfurled, and the vessel steered toward the open ocean.

The artist was overjoyed. He paced by the port rail, rubbing his hands in glee. Melissa hovered over him as if she were his mother, insisting that he don a jacket and a hat. Davina stayed aloof, as she always did, ever vigilant but about as talkative as a clam.

Fargo had assumed she would open up to him after what had happened on Nob Hill. Yet when he tried to make small talk, she had treated him as if he were a pest and brushed him off with short, curt answers.

Now, with the prow of the clipper ship cleaving the emerald sea and throwing foamy spray wide in its wake, Fargo walked over to where she stood gazing into the distance. "I'm curious. Do you treat everyone like dirt, or just those your father hires?"

The redhead had on pants again. She also wore a coat that bulged slightly under each arm. "I really wish you would go about your own business and leave me to mine," she said, without looking at him.

"What is your business? Spotting dolphins?"

Davina glanced at him sharply, but there was a twinkle in her eyes. "I should think you would have guessed by now. It's my job to make sure that no harm comes to my father or my sister. I'm their bodyguard, you might say. And I take my work seriously."

Fargo leaned on the rail and admired how the wind tossed her scarlet locks. "Is this your father's brainstorm of your own?"

"What difference does it make?" Davina said. "Our travels take us to places most sensible people would shun. At one time of another we've had run-ins with hostile Indians, robbers, drunks, and worse. Since I can handle myself better than they can, I take it on myself to watch over them."

Dawning insight increased Fargo's respect for her. "So you crawl into your shell and never, ever come out?"

"When this is over with and the three of us are safely home in New Jersey, then I'll relax and let down my hair. Not before."

"Damn. That means we'll never get to know each other better," Fargo said. "And that's too bad, because I have a hunch we'll be missing out on something special." He walked off, feeling her gaze boring into him. As he rounded the corner of the forward cabin he nearly collided with Melissa Nuttall, who was bringing painting supplies on deck for her father.

"Why don't you watch where you're going, moron?" she declared. "I swear, when they passed out brains, you were off in the outhouse."

Fargo plastered a smile on his face and doffed his hat. "It's a real joy to run into you again, too, Miss Nuttall. Have I ever told you how much I love your sweet disposition?" Leaning close to her ear, he whispered, "Not to mention that body of yours. It's enough to make a grown man drool." He ambled off, leaving her with her mouth hanging open.

The *Celeste* rode the waves so smoothly that he could have sworn he was treading solid ground. Aft, he stared as San Francisco gradually dwindled. The captain sailed due north once the vessel was clear of the Farallon Islands, hugging the coast as they would all the way to Columbia.

Fargo had been on few sea voyages. This was another treat, and he spent most of his time on deck viewing the scenery they passed. The shoreline varied. At times, rolling green hills came right down to the water's edge. Elsewhere, stark cliffs reared above treacherous shoals. Or he saw sandy beaches swarming with gulls.

Clipper ships were the fastest vessels known to man. In fact, they got their name from the way they clipped off the miles. One such ship had crossed the Atlantic in an unbelievable twelve days. Another had made the run from New York City down around Cape Horn and on up to San Francisco in under three months.

The *Celeste* was typical of her kind. Sleek and swift, she ate up the miles. A journey that would have taken weeks on horseback would take them mere days.

That first night Fargo slept soundly, lulled by the gentle rhythm of the ship. Since the captain had invited the Nuttalls, but not him, to take every meal in his cabin, he didn't see anything of the artist and the women until the middle of the morning. Nuttall had a flush to his cheeks and was in fine spirits.

"We'll be at the Columbia before the week is out!" he exclaimed. "From there it's a short run to where we'll be dropped off. Then it's on to Mount Saint Helens and the blue tanager!"

"Then the hard part begins," Fargo cautioned.

Melissa was listening. "Don't tell me that you're afraid of a little hard work?" she baited him.

"No, ma'am," Fargo said. "There are only two things in this world I'm afraid of."

"And what might they be?"

"Being bit by a rabid animal, and a woman with marrying on her mind," Fargo confessed. "Of course, in your case I don't have anything to worry about. The way you go around scaring off every man you meet with that sword you call a tongue, it's plain you don't plan to marry until you're sixty, if then." He got out of there before she could collect her wits and ventured into the hold to give the stallion a brushing. The pinto showed no signs of being seasick, and he spent the better part of an hour walking it in circles to give it exercise. As he came to a stop, he sensed rather than heard someone behind him, and spun.

Davina Nuttall had a bag of feed and was entering the enclosure. "You like that horse a lot, don't you?" she commented.

Fargo patted the Ovaro's neck. "This critter and I have been to hell and back more times than I care to count. I wouldn't part with him for all the gold in California."

"Then you can't be as bad as my little sister claims. Any man who loves animals has to have some good in him."

"Has she decided yet whether she'll shoot me or just slit my throat?"

The redhead laughed. "Quite the opposite. Don't let on I told you, but Melissa is growing real fond of you."

"Is the salt air getting to her?"

"Not hardly. It's been ages since any man had the gumption to stand up to her the way you do. She admires that, even if she won't admit it. If you're not careful, she might try to take you back East with us once Father is done with his painting."

Fargo looked toward the companionway. "Speaking of which, where are they? I thought you didn't let them out of your sight."

"Father is in his cabin sketching, and Melissa is keeping an eye on him while I attend to the horses." Davina draped the feed bag over one of their animals. "I had no idea you would be down here." She had a currycomb which she applied to the mare, her movements as fluid as flowing water. Her buttocks jiggled nicely when she rose on tiptoe and stroked.

A familiar twitch in Fargo's groin reminded him of how long it had been since he last shared a bed with a woman. But he couldn't just walk on over to Davina and put his arms around her to get things started, as he could have done with Greta. She might pull a gun and shoot him.

Still, as the old saw went, where there was a will, there was a way. And Fargo had learned long ago that sometimes the key to stoking a woman's interest was to give her the chance to make the first move. He walked over and watched her a minute, until she turned.

"Don't you have something better to do than to ogle my body?"

"Not that I can think of offhand," Fargo said. "But don't let that stop you from working. Pretend I'm not here."

"I might as well pretend I don't have clothes on."

Fargo smirked. "Now there's an idea." She lifted the comb as if to toss it at him, then abruptly took a step and kissed him hard. It was a brief, fierce kiss. When she broke it, she licked her lips as if savoring the taste. "What was that for?" he asked.

"You already know," Davina said in her sultriest voice. "Damn you all to hell."

They were alone in the hold. Fargo had no qualms about pulling her close and lowering his mouth to hers. She arched her spine and pressed her hands against his chest as if to resist, but once they made contact she ground into him as if trying to climb inside his skin, while her silken tongue glided into his mouth and danced with his. There was an intensity to her passion that kindled his own to raging proportions. In the blink of an eye he was as hard as iron.

Davina scanned the hold, then grabbed his hands and pulled him toward the high stacks of hay in the corner. In the center was a narrow aisle. Davina led him down it to a spot where several bales had been removed and the floor was covered with a layer of loose hay. Suddenly hooking a foot behind him, she pushed.

Fargo braced himself for his fall and then sat there, dazzled by her beauty and astounded by her hunger, as she sank to her knees in front of him. He had seldom met a woman so aggressive. She embraced him and ran her lips over his mouth, his cheeks, his neck. Her breath was warm on his skin; her touch made him tingle.

Davina's eyelids were hooded when she drew back, looked down, and reached for his belt. Fargo tried to undo the buckle himself but she swatted his arm aside and tugged. Once his pants were loose, her hand darted lower.

The feel of her hot fingers on his organ was enough to bring Fargo's blood to a boil. He leaned back as she stroked him. She was much too rough but he was not about to complain and spoil the moment. Her mouth closed on his. He abruptly covered her right breast, then squeezed.

"Damn you!" Davina breathed, stiffening in raw desire.

Fargo could feel her nipple hardening. He tweaked it, then the other one. All the while she was busy below his waist, raising his desire to new heights. Slipping his hand up under her shirt, he found her glorious globes straining for release. She growled deep in her throat and clamped her lips to his.

One of the horses nickered but Fargo paid it no mind. No one could see them back there. And it was doubtful any of the crew would stray among the stacks. He slid his other hand between the redhead's long legs and pressed against her womanhood.

Davina froze, her cherry-red lips parted in a seductive oval, her hand resting lightly on his rigid pole. She closed her eyes and let out a long sigh of sheer contentment. As he cupped her core, she wriggled, smiled, and ground herself into his palm.

Fargo was so aroused he could barely stand it. Normally he liked to pace himself, to have lovemaking last as long as it could. But she had him so inflamed that even though she still had all her clothes on, he was ready to explode in his pants.

Removing her hand, Davina pushed against his chest until he was flat on his back. She swiftly stripped off her coat, exposing a pair of small pistols that she cleverly had fitted into matching holsters nestled under her arms. At another time and place, Fargo would have been more interested in her hideouts, but all he could think of was her luscious body. Hiking her shirt high enough, he loosened her underthings to gain access to her breasts. Her nipples sprang free and he raised his mouth to them.

At the first flick of his tongue, Davina groaned. She pressed on the back of his head, mashing his mouth against her bosom. He accommodated by licking and sucking until she quivered with carnal desire.

Meanwhile, Fargo slipped a hand into her pants. They fit loosely, so he had no problem easing his fingers to her innermost core. She was as hot as an inferno, as wet as water. He rubbed her tiny pleasure button and she bucked and smacked her lips. His middle finger slid into her depths. She ran her hands through his hair, knocking off his hat in the process.

Fargo had a wildcat on his hands. The redhead gave as good as she got, thrusting her body in time to the pumping of his hand. Her fingernails gouged into his shoulders. And when she lowered her face to his, she bit his earlobe so hard that he felt blood trickle down his neck.

"Take your time," Fargo advised. "I'm not going anywhere." But if she heard him, she didn't show it. She bit the tip of his chin as well.

Wanting to get on top, Fargo started to swing her to the right. She stopped him by holding his arms fast. Then she pulled at his pants until they were down around his knees.

Rising partway, Davina lowered her own pants and her underwear. Her bush was as red as the hair above and stood out in bright contrast to her pale skin. She raised herself onto her knees, gripped his member to adjust the angle, and slid down onto him as neatly as she pleased, burying him to the hilt inside of her. A gasp burst from her and she shook as if cold.

Fargo could barely think straight. Rampant lust came over him. His pole pounded with every beat of his heart, and he feared that he would not be able to hold himself back. She didn't help matters any by running her mouth over his face and her hands over every square inch of corded muscle she could reach.

Unexpectedly, Davina took control again by rocking up and down on her knees. She would slide to the tip of his member, then reverse herself. Over and over and over she did it. The friction brought them both to the very pinnacle of self-control.

Fargo's skin was on fire. Every breath seared his lungs with heat. He gave up trying to flip her over and let her do as she pleased, since that was how she wanted it. Her hands shifted to his chest. She propped them there for leverage as she pumped faster than ever. A low moan wafted from deep within her and she gave a convulsive series of shakes, then drove herself into him as if striving to break him in half.

He knew the signs. Holding onto her hips, he held himself in as she spurted. It as as violent a climax as he had ever seen, in keeping with her lovemaking. She would have cried out had she not bitten down on her arm so hard that she broke the skin. It seemed as if she went on convulsing forever. At last she uttered a half sob and started to sag.

That was Fargo's cue. He grabbed her shoulders before she could stop him and held her in place, even as he whipped his hips up off the hay. Her eyes widened. She twisted, trying to wrestle loose, but he was not to be denied. Driving himself way up into her, he hammered away until his own explosion came with the suddenness and jolt of a lightning bolt.

"Damn you! Damn you!" Davina growled, reaching another summit of her own. She punched at him, lightly. Her hips matched his, motion for motion.

Their bodies fused as one, Fargo and the redhead coasted to a gradual stop. Both were breathing hard and were caked with sweat. She began to sink onto his chest but caught herself and straightened. Rising, she had to support herself against the bales or her legs would have given out.

"What's your hurry?" Fargo asked as she adjusted her clothes and picked up her coat.

Instead of answering, Davina looked at him and said, "You make me feel all weak inside." She moved slowly to the aisle. "And I hate feeling weak."

Just like that, she was gone. Fargo opened his mouth to call her but thought better of the notion. She was a strong-willed, independent woman. If her passion for him upset her, it was a problem she had to deal with on her own. Nothing he could say or do would soothe her.

Stretching, Fargo propped his hands behind his head and re- laxed. Once they reached Washington Territory, rest was a luxury he would not be able to afford. He was on the verge of dozing off when another horse whinnied. This time he sat up and took notice, because it was the Ovaro that made the noise.

Having traveled from one end of the country to the other on that stallion, Fargo knew its voice as well as he knew his own. He knew the sound it made when it was content, the sound it made when it was agitated, and the sound it made when some- thing wasn't quite right. Such as now.

Rising, Fargo hitched his pants and buckled his belt. Since leaving port he had strapped his Colt around his waist and never went anywhere without it. Drawing the pistol, he prowled between the stacks and scoured the hold from one end to the other. No one was there.

The Ovaro was gazing at the companionway. Fargo guessed that whoever had been there had gone. Possibly it had been a crewman on an assigned task.

Twirling the six-shooter into its holster, Fargo gave the pinto a last pat and climbed to the upper deck. The sun felt warm on his face. The sea breeze was as tangy as ever.

William Nuttall and his daughters were coming out of the painter's cabin. Nuttall smiled and waved. So, to Fargo's amusement, did Melissa. Davina turned her back on him.

Taking that as a hint, Fargo stepped to the starboard side

and walked aft. As he passed the pilothouse two men came out. In the lead was Captain Gibson. The other man happened to be one of the three who had arrived late the day the ship sailed.

Gibson was saying testily, "No, damn your bones! Not on my ship, you won't! I don't care how much—" He stopped short on seeing Fargo, and blurted, "By Davy Jones's beard, you're quiet on your feet, sir! I didn't hear you coming."

"I didn't mean to spook you," Fargo said. The other man had turned and was hurrying off. "I've spent so much time in the wilds that it's a habit with me."

Gibson pushed his cap back on his head and squinted one eye. "You must be something of an Injun fighter, then?"

"I've tangled with a few," Fargo allowed.

"Rather you than me, friend," the captain said. "I've had a dread of heathens ever since my sainted grandfather was butchered and scalped by Paiutes." Gibson consulted a vest watch. "We're making good time, if I do say so myself. But I must say, I hope you folks know what you're doing. I have reservations about dropping you off in the middle of nowhere. The savages in that part of the country are not very friendly."

"We'll manage," Fargo replied.

Gibson shifted to leave, then paused. "Say, did you happen to hear the news before we left San Francisco?"

"What news?"

Giving Fargo an odd look, the seaman said, "About the fuss at the Nob Hill Country Club. A man by the name of Scaglia was killed, and a few others wounded." Snapping the watch-case shut, he mentioned, "Scaglia is no loss to humanity. They say he was one of the worst criminals in the city."

Fargo did not say a word.

"The problem with a man like, though, is that he can be just as dangerous dead as he was alive. He's like a big, nasty octopus, with tentacles reaching all over the place. A man never knows but when one of those tentacles might catch hold of him and squeeze until he's drained of life. Don't you think?"

"I suppose," Fargo said. Gibson smiled and departed, leaving him to wonder what that had been all about. Could it be, he mused, that the captain knew he was to blame? The idea seemed preposterous, since the only person who did know was Davina, and he trusted her not to confide in a soul. Had it been a warning of some kind, then? If so, he decided it would be best if he stuck close to the Nuttalls for the rest of the trip.

The afternoon waxed and waned. Fargo kept the artist and his daughters in sight at all times without being obvious about it. But nothing happened. Evening came, and the family repaired to the captain's cabin for their supper.

Fargo returned to his own cabin, where a tray of food was waiting. Sea air, he had found, made him ravenous, so he downed every last morsel and drank three cups of hot black coffee. A crewman came for the plates and silverware.

Afterward, as a mantel of darkness descended on the Pacific, Fargo went for a stroll. He sauntered toward the bow and had just passed the forecastle when a heavy body slammed onto him from above, bearing him to the deck. The attack was so swift that he was on his stomach, stunned, before he knew what had happened. He barely felt it when steely fingers seized him by the hair and snapped his head back. But he did see the long blade that materialized in front of his eyes.

He was about to have his throat slit!

6

The sight of the blade cleared Skye Fargo's head as nothing else could have. As it slashed toward his neck, he lunged and seized his attacker's wrist. With a powerful heave of his broad shoulders, he swung the man around in front of him. It took the would-be murderer off guard. The man tripped over Fargo's back, stumbled, and fell to one knee, while Fargo simultaneously rose onto his own.

It was a seaman. That was all Fargo could tell by his assailant's clothes. Darkness shrouded the man's face, except for the feral flash of teeth as he hissed and stabbed.

Fargo twisted, evading the knife. His hand flashed to his Colt, but as he drew the seaman swung again, and whether by accident or design the blade struck the pistol, sending it skidding across the deck. Fargo jerked back as the knife sought his heart. He wanted to draw his own knife, but his leg was tucked under him and he couldn't get at his boot.

The man closed, his right arm upraised. Fargo held his ground, clamping his hand on the killer's forearm to keep the blow from landing. Locked together, grunting and straining, they grappled. The attacker was strong, but so was Fargo. His whipcord frame packed solid muscle from head to toe, sinews he now used to slowly bend the seaman's right arm backward until it was about to snap.

Uttering a low cry, the seaman frantically tore loose and pushed to his feet. Fargo surged after him, freeing the Arkansas toothpick as he straightened. He met the next cut with a parry. Their blades clinked.

"Bastard!" the man growled, and redoubled his efforts. Crouching, he wielded his weapon with exceptional skill.

Anyone less experienced than Fargo would have fallen then and there. He waged a glittering defense, countering strike after strike. Circling first to the right, then to the left, bit by bit he backed the seaman toward the port rail.

The man glanced back, deduced his strategy, and fought with renewed fury.

Fargo kept expecting to hear a shout or the pounding of feet as others came on the run to see what was going on. He had to remind himself that very few of the crew were ever on deck at that time of day. Most were lounging in their quarters, while the captain and the Nuttalls were probably chatting over glasses of sherry or brandy. His attacker had picked the most opportune moment to jump him.

They were almost to the railing. The seaman stopped retreating and speared his knife at Fargo's stomach. Pivoting, Fargo felt a slight tug on his shirt. Then his own blade sliced deep into the man's shoulder.

Automatically the killer hurled himself to the rear. In doing so he miscalculated. He struck the rail so hard that he lost his balance. His feet left the deck as he started to go over the side. He released the knife to clutch at the rail with both hands, but it was too late.

Fargo took a bound and grasped at the man's leg. He needed his attacker alive to find out why he had been jumped. His fingers caught hold of the man's pants, but he couldn't get a firm enough grip to prevent the inevitable.

Gravity took over. The man made one last desperate attempt to grip the edge of the deck, then he plummeted. He didn't scream or shout for help or curse. He simply fell straight as a rock.

Fargo leaped to the rail and saw his attacker hit the surface with a resounding splash. The impact was much too close to the hull, almost under the keel, and the man was sucked under. He didn't come up again. Fargo marked the impact point, never taking his eyes off it, leaning as far out as he dared. He was going to yell to alert the crew so they could fish the seaman out of the drink. Then the clipper cleared the spot and a few seconds later the body bobbed to the surface.

There could be no doubt the man was dead. He was face-down, his arms flung out. It was difficult to see, but part of his head appeared to have been caved in.

Disappointed, Fargo stepped back. His foot bumped the killer's knife. He picked it up, then replaced the toothpick, reclaimed his Colt, and stormed toward the captain's cabin. In the mood he was in, he never considered knocking. Working the latch, he slammed the door wide open and barged in on Gibson and his guests.

They were startled half out of their wits, with one exception. The captain jumped in his chair and paused in the act of tipping a glass of brandy to his lips. William Nuttall blurted, "My word!" and nearly dropped his own drink. Melissa gasped, pressing a hand to her throat. Only Davina stayed calm and collected. She started to go for the pistols under her coat but stopped when she saw who it was.

Fargo stormed up to the table. Glaring at Gibson, he embedded the attacker's knife in the wood within inches of the captain's belly. "I want to know what the hell is going on, and I want to know *now*."

Gibson acted genuinely shocked. Setting his brandy down, he declared, "See here! What is the meaning of this outrage? What are you raving about?"

"One of your men just tried to kill me," Fargo rasped, and detailed the attempt. "I'd like to know why."

The captain turned beet-red from his neck to his receding hairline. "Preposterous!" he bellowed. "My crew is the best in the business. None of them would resort to—" Suddenly he caught himself, blinked a few times, and swallowed. Recovering, he finished by saying in a level tone, "If someone attacked you, it must have been a stowaway."

Fargo didn't believe the man for a second and told Gibson as much.

"I can prove it," the sea wolf said. "As I told you the first day out, I have twenty-nine hands working under me. Come

66

with me to their quarters and we'll see if one is missing. But there won't be."

"Lead the way," Fargo directed.

Gibson donned his cap, clasped his hands behind his back, and stalked out. Fargo glued himself to the captain's side, heedless of the Nuttalls, who trailed along. They burst into the crew's cabin unannounced, and to say the men were flabbergasted would have been an understatement. Fully half were lying on their bunks in various stages of undress. Five were playing cards. Two had a game of dominoes going.

Without offering to explain why, Captain Gibson ordered them to line up in two rows. He went down the middle, counting them off in a loud voice. Twenty-four were present.

Fargo looked at him. "You claimed twenty-nine."

"I keep a man in the crow's nest every hour of the day. Two more are assigned to the wheelhouse at all times. And the cook and young Stenmeyer aren't here, so they must be cleaning up the kitchen."

"Let's check on all of them," Fargo proposed, certain one would be missing.

But none were. A pair of seamen were indeed in the wheelhouse, the cook and a young hand were washing pots and pans, and when Gibson walked to the base of the mainmast to hail the crow's nest, a man answered. Gibson asked if the lookout had seen anything out of the ordinary. Loud and clear came the answer. "No, sir!"

Fargo glanced toward the bow. From where the lookout roosted, the man could not have seen the fight. Intervening sails and the forecastle blocked that part of the deck from view, which the attacker must have known.

"Satisfied?" Gibson asked smugly.

"Not by a long shot," Fargo said. "The one who jumped me wore seaman's clothes. Who else could it have been, if not one of your men?"

Gibson sighed. "Unlike some captains I could name, I don't hire riffraff, sir. My crew are all decent, hardworking sorts, not murderers and thieves. And every man jack of them knows that if he makes trouble on my ship, he'll swing by his thumbs from the yardarm or have the skin on his back flayed off by my whip."

There was no denying his sincerity, but Fargo still harbored doubts.

"Don't be so quick to discount my stowaway idea," Gibson continued. "Men are sneaking onto ships all the time. Some want to get somewhere but don't have the fare. Others are criminals fleeing the law. My guess is that the man who tried to kill you was a common footpad." Gesturing toward the stern, he said, "Just look at the size of the *Celeste*. She's hundreds of feet long and higher than a building. There are plenty of places a man could hide."

Fargo couldn't dispute that. "If you're right, maybe you should have your men go over her from top to bottom. I don't want any more nasty surprises."

"Consider it done." Gibson started to leave, then hesitated. "I truly am sorry this happened. Rest assured that the safety of your party will be my main concern for the duration of our short voyage." Doffing his cap to the ladies, he bent his steps to the crew's quarters.

Davina Nuttall walked up. "Do you believe him?" she asked softly.

"I don't know what to believe," Fargo admitted. It was just possible that the man *had* been a stowaway. But that raised the question of whether the attack had been random or someone had put the cutthroat up to it. And if someone had, who? The logical suspect was Bruno Scaglia, but he was dead. Fargo could think of no one else in San Francisco who might want him dead.

"From here on out, I'm not leaving my father's side," Davina announced.

"Good idea," Fargo said. "When you turn in tonight, I'd advise you to shove a chair in front of your door. Not one has a lock."

The painter and his other daughter joined them. "I must say," Nuttall stated, "I find this whole business rather unsavory. An acquaintance assured me that Captain Gibson was a reputable man and his ship one of the best run, or I would never have chartered it."

Melissa drew her shawl tight around her. "Where there's one killer there might be more. Now I won't be able to sleep well until we're safely on shore."

Fargo didn't point out that once they began the overland stage of their journey, the dangers would multiply. "I just hope the rest of the voyage goes smoothly," he said.

It didn't. Late the next afternoon, rolling dark clouds appeared to the northwest. Captain Gibson took one look and proceeded to bawl out orders. "We're in for a gale," he roared for the sake of his passengers. "Get in your cabins and batten down the hatches while we ride it out."

For the seamen it was business as usual. They had weathered countless storms and swiftly went about their assigned tasks. Some swarmed up the masts to attend to the rigging and sails, while others scurried about the deck lashing down anything and everything that might be washed overboard.

Fargo went below. All the shouting and drumming of feet had the horses agitated. He calmed them as best he could. Soon, though, the wind picked up, howling past the top of the hold like a demented banshee. The animals nickered and pranced nervously about. He quickly fashioned hobbles from a coil of rope, then slid one on each animal, even the Ovaro.

The precaution proved worth it. Presently rain began to pelt the ship and the sea commenced to churn. Where before the *Celeste* had glided along as if over glass, now the vessel rocked and bucked as if sailing over a bed of boulders. The horses were terrified. Several tried to break out of the enclosure. Others reared and plunged but could not do much damage to the ship or themselves thanks to the hobbles.

The hold darkened to the point where Fargo could barely see his hand when he extended an arm. He stumbled from horse to horse, the rocking motion of the hull threatening to pitch him onto his face. No sooner would he briefly calm one animal than another would act up. Again and again he made the rounds.

Outside, thunder rumbled, lightning flared. Flashes lit up the hold as regularly as clockwork. At one point Fargo happened to be facing the companionway and thought that he saw a vague figure rapidly descending. The light died out. At the next flash he looked again, but no one was there.

His eyes could have been playing tricks on him. Given the attempt on his life, however, Fargo was not about to take chances. He crouched between two of the horses and scoured the shadows.

In addition to the hay, expedition supplies and other goods ringed the enclosure. Bathed in the flickering glow of Mother Nature's tantrums, they stood out in stark relief. Behind a stack of crates, something moved. A spectral shape flitted to a collection of farm equipment bound for Olympia.

Fargo palmed his Colt and thumbed back the hammer. He had a feeling that whoever was out there hadn't spotted him yet. The milling horses and the makeshift rope corral disguised him well.

Then the biggest bolt of all rent the heavens above, illuminating the hold as brightly as the sun would. In that instant a smaller flash split the air, and a slug thudded into the floor at Fargo's feet. He responded in kind, two swift shots that spanged off a plow. The assassin ducked down.

Diving, Fargo rolled a dozen feet until he came up against the enclosure. He flattened just as the figure burst from concealment and darted toward a mound of trade goods. Fargo fired once but knew he missed. The man's answering shot was just as wild. Before either of them could squeeze the trigger again, the figure reached cover.

Fargo crawled forward. Behind some crates he eased up into a crouch. He figured the man would try to sneak closer, and he was ready. The next flash, though, revealed no one. After that the hold was dark for quite some time.

It was nerve-racking, hunkered there in the gloom, never knowing when the shooter might pop up and blaze away. Between the racket raised by the horses and the din of the storm, he couldn't hear himself think, let alone hear footsteps.

The Ovaro saved his life by suddenly whinnying long and loud. Fargo looked to see why and spied a black form over by the hay. There was a muzzle flash, then another. At each retort the air near his ear zinged with the passage of hot lead. Fargo fanned the Colt, emptying the cylinder and driving the man to cover.

Springing to the left, Fargo ran the length of the corral and vaulted over the top rope. He landed lightly in the shelter of a stack of long crates. It took a moment to reload and on he went, working along to where he could see the hay clearly.

The *Celeste* was not rocking as badly as she had been earlier, and the patter or rain on the hull had tapered off. Soon the storm would abate, the sky would clear. Fargo intended to keep the gunman pinned down until then. He covered both sides, his senses primed. The minutes dragged by. At length the hold brightened as stray shafts of sunshine filtered down.

The bushwhacker never showed himself.

Somehow, the man had given Fargo the slip. He checked the hold from stem to stern and turned up no one. After removing the hobbles so the horses could move freely, he climbed to the upper deck where the seamen were rigging for the short run that remained to their destination.

Fargo did not even consider telling Gibson. The good captain would just blame another stowaway or concoct some other story. He moved over near the rail to be out of the way and studied the members of the crew in the vain hope that the culprit would give himself away by a nervous glance or a spiteful look or some other act.

Not long after the rain stopped, the Nuttalls emerged. William sucked in the dank air and thumped his chest, saying, "Lord, I love the ocean! It puts vigor in a man's veins. Don't you agree, Skye?"

"Vigor or lead," Fargo said, but the remark went right over the artist's head.

"I fancy a stroll after being cooped up the past few hours," the painter said. "Anyone care to tag along?"

Melissa did. Davina told them she would catch up, and as soon as they were out of earshot she turned. "What was that business about lead?"

Keeping it short and sweet, Fargo told her. "Whoever it

was," he concluded, "was a damn good shot. As dark as it was, with the whole ship tossing like a flapjack on a griddle, he nearly blew my head off."

"You'd better be extra careful," the redhead said. "Whoever is after you doesn't have much time left before we're put ashore. They're bound to try again."

Fargo agreed. From then on he always kept his back to the open sea when outdoors and always shoved furniture in front of his door when he was in his cabin. He slept with the Colt in hand. And every time he ventured into the hold, he took his big Henry rifle.

It was a cloudy day, about nine in the morning, when the wide mouth of the mighty Columbia hove into sight. At a bellow from the lookout, all the hands spilled onto the upper deck and prepared to navigate the waterway.

Captain Gibson moved to the bow, standing near Fargo. Several seamen took up posts on either side to watch for reefs and submerged boulders. Another used a plumb line with a metal bob at the end to take regular depth readings. Once they were safely in the main channel, they flashed past Astoria, a settlement on the south coast. In due course, after negotiating several bends, they sailed on by Portland, the only city Fargo had ever heard of to get its name as the result of a coin toss. According to the story, the two founding fathers had argued over whether to call it Portland—or Boston.

William Nuttall grew more and more excited the farther they went. He had studied his maps well and knew just where he wanted to land. When the inlet appeared, he actually bounced up and down with joy. He reminded Fargo of a small boy who had been granted his heart's desire.

It took some skillful steering on the part of the wheelman to bring the clipper ship around and into the wind. Captain Gibson drifted in close enough to lower the gangplank.

Fargo had his hands full for over an hour, unloading the horses and supplies. One of the pack animals balked at going down and had to be prodded and pulled before it would budge. As it was, he had the stubborn horse over halfway to the bottom when it decided it would rather swim, and over the side of the gangplank it went. He had the reins looped around a wrist at the time. Before he could unwind them, he was jerked into the air. One of the women shouted his name.

The drop was short but the river deep. Cold, dark water enclosed Fargo in a clammy sheath as he sank. He tried to break his descent by kicking furiously, but the weight of the thrashing horse dragged him lower. He glimpsed the murky bottom and was about to cast the reins off when something buffeted him with so much force that he was nearly swept away.

It was the current. Fargo had heard several of the crew talk about the strong current in the Columbia, but he had never imagined it would be as fierce as it was. If not for the horse serving to anchor him, he would have been flung back toward the sea as if shot from a cannon. Instead of unraveling the reins, he held on tight and flung an arm over the animal's back as it rose to the surface. The horse immediately struck out for shore. Grabbing its tail, he let it do all the work. Which was only fair, in his opinion, since the four-legged knothead was responsible for their tumble.

The Nuttall clan, Captain Gibson, and several crew members were on hand to help Fargo clamber from the water. He was soaked to the skin and could not stop shivering. Previous mishaps had taught him the wisdom of always having a spare set of buckskins on hand. In this case they were worn and needed mending at the seams, but they would do until his good ones dried out.

Finally everything had been unloaded. The captain shook hands with the artist and gave each of the women a polite peck on the cheek. Then he stood before Fargo.

"More than likely you won't believe me, but I truly am sorry about the attempt on your life. Surely a man like you can understand that sometimes things happen over which we have no control. Take this harebrained expedition. Nuttall has no idea what's in store. You're facing some of the worst terrain on the face of the earth. There are savages in there who will leap at the chance to separate you from your hides. Not to mention hungry grizzlies and the like. All things over which you have no control—yet you're going anyway."

Fargo did not quite see what the captain was getting at, but he accepted the man's hand anyway.

"Keep your eyes peeled," Gibson said. Strangely enough, he repeated it with more emphasis. "*Keep your eyes peeled.*"

"We will," Fargo said, and was puzzled by the relief mirrored in the other's eyes.

A moment later the painter came over to bid the captain farewell. "Thanks again for everything. And you will remember to deliver my message to Cavendar? He needs to know that we've arrived safely."

"Of course," Gibson pledged.

Ira Cavendar operated a ferry service in Portland. Nuttall had contacted the man weeks before, asking that Cavendar be on the watch for the signal fire they would build on their return from Mount Saint Helens. It was Fargo's job to bring them out close to the north shore opposite the city.

The captain and his men went on board. The gangplank was hoisted. Sails were unfurled. Majestically knifing westward, the *Celeste* soon became a mere speck.

"At last!" Nuttall exclaimed with glee. "Now our grand adventure truly begins!"

Skye Fargo glanced at the swift dark water in front of them, then at the low gray clouds overhead and the ominous tangle of vegetation behind them. He could think of many ways to describe the ordeal they were in for.

"Grand adventure" wasn't one of them.

7

The Nuttalls found that out for themselves soon enough.

Since plenty of daylight remained, Fargo led them due north shortly after the clipper ship was gone. A steep bank brought them to the summit of a low hill. Ahead were more hills, only these were higher. Beyond reared the formidable mountains of the Cascade Range. Among them, its summit rimmed by snow, towered Mount Saint Helens. Loftier still was the crown of Mount Rainier, the highest peak in the whole territory, visible far to the northeast.

Fargo headed down the hill. Almost immediately he had to contend with thick tangles of vegetation that made traveling in a straight line for any length of time impossible. He constantly had to detour around obstacles. Ravines and gullies had to be crossed with great care since stones and loose earth constantly slid out from under the horses' hooves. Briars grew rampant in areas, sporting big thorns so sharp that being jabbed by them was like being stabbed by miniature daggers.

As if all that were not enough of a headache, the party had to deal with a steady heavy rain. The clouds unleashed the first large, cold drops about an hour after they left the Columbia, and it was still raining at twilight when Fargo called a halt. While the others set up camp, he went in search of game and dropped a bounding rabbit at forty yards. Presently he had a tangy stew boiling in their cook pot.

The women had tended to the horses, tethering the animals for the night and stripping the pack animals. When they came over to the fire, they were both exhausted. The deluge had soaked both to the skin and their clothes clung damply to their bodies, leaving little to the imagination.

"Is it going to be like this the whole trip?" Melissa wondered wearily. "Only half a day in the saddle and I'm ready to keel over."

"It will get worse," Fargo warned them.

William Nuttall bounced up, smacking his lips. "I say, Fargo, that smells delicious! I had no idea when I retained your services that skill as a cook was one of your many talents."

Fargo had to marvel at the man's boundless energy. The painter had worked just as hard as any of them, yet still managed to chatter on like a chipmunk the entire afternoon, pointing out bird after bird and going on at great length about the known habits of each. He ladled some stew onto a tin plate and handed it to Nuttall. "Eat hearty. You'll need all your strength tomorrow."

The rain had slackened to a drizzle. Sheltered by the limbs of an overspreading pine, Fargo and his companions were snug and comfortable. He nodded at a low branch and suggested the women hang their clothes up to dry overnight.

"I'll trust you'll be a gentleman and look the other way when we undress?" Melissa asked stiffly.

"I'll look away, but I can't promise I won't peek."

About to take a bite of rabbit, Melissa scrunched up her nose at him and remarked, "As crude as ever, I see. With the lousy manners you have, you must have no luck at all with women. I'd wager that you haven't been with one in so long, you've forgotten what it's like."

Her father made a clucking noise and wagged a finger in disapproval, while Davina pretended to be interested in a clod of mud sticking to the side of her boot.

Fargo could not help but grin. "Oh, I've known one or two in my time." He put on an air of fake innocence and smiled. "It's awful nice of you to be so concerned about my love life. I didn't know you cared."

"I don't!" Melissa said, much too sharply.

"No need to deny it," Fargo said. "No one here will hold it

against you if you come right out and admit that you just can't wait to get your hands on me."

The raven-haired beauty shot to her feet and made as if to hurl her plate at him. The only thing that stopped her was the mirth of her father and sister. Melissa glared at each of them in turn, then stomped her foot and said, "My own family! I should think you would stand up for my virtue instead of letting this ruffian poke fun at me."

William Nuttall snickered. "As our friend here might say, climb down off your high horse and sit down. Mr. Fargo is just giving you a taste of your own medicine. Be woman enough to take it in stride."

"Father!"

"Oh, cut it out!" Nuttall declared with a hint of irritation. "If you go around treating people like dirt, sooner or later you must expect to have some flung back in your face." He smacked the ground. "Now, sit, damn it, and quit making a spectacle of yourself."

The younger sister obeyed. But if looks could kill, the gaze she threw Fargo's way would have dropped him on the spot. "Have your fun while you can, primitive. But I assure you that I would rather mate with a monkey than with you."

On that happy note everyone lapsed into silence. Fargo finished off two heaping helpings plus two cups of black coffee. Nearby lay the pack that contained the artist's paints, brushes, and other supplies, and on noticing it, he recalled the time several years ago when he had arrived at Fort Benton up on the Missouri River and found a Dutch painter there capturing the local Indians on canvas. As he recollected, it had taken that Dutchman a week and a half to do one portrait. If Nuttall was just as slow, their expedition could end up taking a lot longer than he had counted on. Turning to Nuttall, he said, "Tell me something. Once we find a blue tanager, how long will it take for you to finish your painting?"

"Three or four days, at the most. I like to work quickly, while the memory is fresh."

"We have only enough supplies to last us two weeks,"

Fargo mentioned. "Let's hope we come across one before then."

"I'm sure we will." Nuttall brimmed with confidence. "I've never failed yet." He chortled. "As I'm fond of saying, I always get my bird."

Fargo left the peculiar little man and walked off to give the Ovaro a rubdown. As he stroked the brush, he listened to the night sounds all around them. To the northwest, wolves howled; to the east, a lone coyote yipped. Deep in the forest an owl voiced the ageless question of its kind. Elsewhere a mountain lion screamed. Then he heard someone come up behind him.

"You've done it now," Davina said. "Don't blame me if she's all over you the first chance she gets."

"What are you talking about?"

"Poor Melissa. She's all hot and bothered. It's a wonder she can keep her hands off you, after you put her in her place like you did." Davina shook her head. "I don't know how, but you sure have a knack for making women fall head over heels for you."

Fargo glanced toward the fire, where Melissa continued to glare at him as if she couldn't wait to stuff burning coals down his throat while he slept. "I must have missed something somewhere along the line."

"Oh, don't play coy with me," Davina said. "I wasn't born yesterday. You planned all along to get her mad at you so she'd want to give you a tumble in the grass. Just like you paid no attention to me at first, knowing it would only make me more interested in you."

For the life of him, Fargo failed to see her logic. "If I live to be a hundred," he muttered, "I will never, ever understand women."

The rest of the night passed peacefully. Since there had been no sign of Indians or roving grizzlies, Fargo saw no need to have them take turns standing watch. He let the others curl up close to the fire but spread his own bedroll near the horses, where a nicker from the Ovaro would bring him to his feet in a hurry. Stretching out on his back, he pulled the Colt and slid it between his blanket and his stomach, ready for instant use.

The drizzle did not let up once. Fargo fell asleep to the muffled patter of tiny drops, and the same patter was the first sound he heard on awakening at the crack of dawn.

Coffee and leftover stew sufficed for their breakfast. Fargo saddled the horses and had help from Davina in loading the packs. As they rode out, the rain increased again and stayed a steady downpour until noon. Fargo was wet to the bone in no time. The best he could do was pull his hat brim low and hunch his shoulders to keep the rain from dripping down inside his shirt. He would have given anything for a slicker, but he had not brought one west with him. His mistake.

Neither of the women spoke much. It was Melissa's turn to ride at the rear, leading the pack animals, and she had her hands full, what with slippery slopes and briars and fording swift streams. Davina had fashioned a poncho from a spare blanket. While it didn't keep her dry, it spared her from the worst of the deluge.

William Nuttall, as before, was like a hungry kid surrounded by sweetmeats, unable to decide which one to pick. All day long they ran into birds. Each time, the painter would begin a long-winded spiel about the specimen in question, only to cut himself short seconds or minutes later when he spotted a different kind. Then he would start in again. Over and over this happened, until Fargo was so sick of hearing about birds he hankered to shoot the next one he saw.

Fargo's eyes scoured the ground often. About the middle of the afternoon he discovered bear tracks, but they were three days old and their size told him they had been made by a black bear, not a grizzly. There was no trace of Indian activity.

Much of their time was spent traveling through ages-old forest, where broad trees towered high overhead and a spongy carpet of pine needles cushioned the noise their mounts made. Moss was everywhere—growing on trunks, on branches, even on rocks and boulders. Ferns were also abundant.

That night Fargo made camp on the north bank of the Lewis River. He forded before dark so they would be ready to go at first light and picked a spot where fallen pines formed a natural giant lean-to. Since they were in a hollow bordered on all four sides by lushly wooded slopes, he made the fire bigger than was his custom so they would dry off that much faster.

Melissa, ever quick to criticize, commented, "Why didn't you do this last night?" She gestured at the forest. "Afraid of running out of wood?"

"We were high on a hill. The fire could have been seen for miles." Fargo turned the makeshift spit on which he was roasting the haunch of a small buck he had shot before dark.

"Who is there to see?" Melissa said. "After all that talk about savages, we haven't come across a single one."

"Count your blessings. Just because you don't see them doesn't mean they're not out there," Fargo said. "I'm taking a risk doing this, but I did it for your sakes."

"How sweet of you."

Fargo looked at her father. "Has anyone ever hauled off and slugged her, just for the hell of it?"

"No." Nuttall grinned, and would have gone on, but just then several of the horses whinnied, among them the stallion.

In a flash, Fargo was over by the string, straining to hear what they heard. The breeze carried with it the faint twitter of another damn bird and the irate chitter of a squirrel whose rest had been disturbed, but that was all. Nothing to explain why the horses had acted up. They were staring off to the west, the pinto's nostrils flaring. So whatever had them spooked was something they had *smelled*, not heard. He sniffed, too. For while his nose was not nearly as sensitive as theirs, if the wind was right, sometimes he could sniff out a circling grizzly. This time, though, all he smelled was the minty scent of the pines and the dank odor of the rich soil.

"Anything?" Davina asked at his elbow.

Fargo had not heard her come up and nearly started. "I wish," he said.

"You do?"

"The secret of staying alive in the wild is to spot your enemies before they spot you. I'd rather know who is out there before they spring a nasty surprise on us."

"It might just be an animal."

"No. Listen closely."

The redhead bent her head. "I am, and all I hear is a bird and a squirrel cursing each other out."

"That's just it. Why are they acting up?" Fargo nodded at the night. "What else do you hear?"

"Not a thing."

"But you should. All kinds of animals. Yet it's as quiet as a tomb. Something is out there, all right. And more than likely it's something that walks on two legs." Fargo went down the line of horses, verifying they were securely tied to the picket pins the artist had brought along. The redhead paced him every step of the way.

"You're saying Indians are out there somewhere?"

"That would be my guess."

"Do you think they know we're here?" Davina asked anxiously, surveying the slopes.

"Not yet, or they would have paid us a visit by now," Fargo responded. "But we'll have to keep our eyes peeled tomorrow." He slowly rose, recalling that those were the exact words Captain Gibson had used on the shore of the Columbia. Was that what the seafarer had meant? Be on the lookout for Indians? Or was there more to it than that?"

"Should one of us stand guard tonight?"

"We'll take turns," Fargo proposed. "All four of us can keep watch for three hours at a stretch."

"Four hours each," Davina amended. "Just Melissa, you, and me. I don't want my father imposed on. He needs his rest."

"That will make it harder for the rest of us," Fargo pointed out. "What harm can it do for him to go a few hours without sleep? Aren't you being too protective?"

"I know he doesn't act it at times, but he's older than both of us combined," Davina said. "All this riding has to be getting to him, wearing him down. So we let him rest as often and as long as he likes. If that upsets you, my sister and I will share his turn."

"That won't be necessary," Fargo said, but he was troubled.

They all had to pull their own weight if they intended to get back to civilization alive.

Nuttall sat up as they returned. "Don't keep us in suspense. What caused the animals to act up?"

Davina answered before Fargo could. "They probably caught the scent of a bobcat or something. It's nothing for you to worry about." She crouched in front of her sister. "But since we can't afford to have any of our stock run off, Fargo and I think it would be a wise idea to have someone awake at all times."

"Excellent suggestion," the artist said. "What time do I sit up with them?"

"You don't. You get to sleep all night long," Davina said. "Remember, you need to be fresh and alert for when we spot the blue tanager."

"But that's not fair to the rest of you."

"We'll manage," Davina told him. He was going to object but she raised a hand. "I don't want to hear it. A long time ago we decided that I have the final say where our safety is concerned. If you won't do as I want, I swear that I'll have Skye turn around and take us to Portland."

The painter was none too happy but he made the best of the situation by winking at Fargo and remarking, "There's a lesson in this, my friend. Never give your offspring an inch or they'll demand a yard."

Both daughters found that funny. Fargo smiled to be polite, but a gnawing doubt festered at the back of his mind. He watched Nuttall more closely from then on and noticed little things he had overlooked before. Such as how the artist always dozed off early, unable to keep his eyes open much past eight. Such as how Nuttall was always the last one out from under the blankets in the morning and had to walk around quite a while to relieve stiffness in his joints and limbs. And how Nuttall had a special fondness for coffee. Out of every pot made, the man drank fully half. By itself, each incident did not mean much. But taken together, they spelled trouble.

It was the middle of the day before Fargo could bring himself to pry. They had stopped in a glade skirted by a creek, and the sisters were watering the horses. He walked over to where Nuttall sat on a log, sketching a hummingbird they had seen flitting about earlier. Nuttall grinned up at him.

"I've painted this one before, but I need regular practice to keep my hand in, as it were."

Fargo did not mince words. "Why didn't you tell me that you're ill?"

The pencil point snapped. Nuttall's mouth fell open, but he quickly closed it and pursed his lips. "My goodness, you're an astute fellow. Or did one of my daughters tell you?"

"They love you too much to do that. They've been protecting your secret the whole time. So what is it? Arthritis? Gout? Rheumatism? Something like that?"

"No, actually," the artist said pleasantly, "it's my heart. It nearly failed on me about eight months ago, and the doctors say it could go out at any time."

Fargo suddenly needed to sit down. He had guessed that the man was ailing, but never in his wildest dreams would he have suspected Nuttall to be *that* bad off. "Are you plumb loco?" he demanded. "Traipsing into these mountains in your condition?"

"It had to be done."

"Like hell," Fargo snapped. "Do you have any notion of the bind you've put us in? Your girls are going to be sick with worry this whole trip, which means they won't be as sharp as they should be. And now I have to take it easy on you so you don't up and drop dead at my feet. We'll have to go slower than we have been. Hell, we'll be lucky if we reach Portland in six weeks."

Nuttall set his pad down and folded his hands. "I don't blame you for being upset. It was terribly remiss of me not to tell you sooner. But I couldn't. You would have declined to guide us if you had known."

"Damn right I would have," Fargo said. "This expedition of yours is dangerous enough as it is. Now I have another headache to add to the list."

"Please don't be mad," Nuttall pleaded. "Hear me out. Once

you do, you'll understand why I insisted on keeping my condition secret."

"I doubt that, but go ahead."

Clearing his throat, Nuttall said softly, "I don't mind that my time is at an end. I really don't. I've had a long, full life, and I have two wonderful daughters to carry on the family name." He paused. "The only regret I have is that I won't be able to track down all the birds I wanted to put on canvas before I gave up the ghost. Art is my life, you see, and birds are my passion."

"Could have fooled me," Fargo said dryly.

Nuttall acted as if he hadn't heard. "I couldn't bear the thought of spending the rest of my days confined to a rocking chair, waiting for the end to come. I wanted to paint one last rare bird, a special bird like the beautiful blue tanager we're after. So I had a long talk with my doctor. He said that if I don't overexert myself, I should be all right."

"*Should* be." Fargo stressed the pertinent part.

"So this expedition is a risk. So what? Life is a risk, isn't it? Every day we wake up with no guarantee that we'll be alive to tuck ourselves in at night. We should make the most of the time allotted us. And that's exactly what I'm doing." Nuttall smiled at his daughters, who waved back. "Do you hold that against me?"

Fargo offered no answer.

"Another thing, Skye. I wanted one more outing with my girls. They mean so much to me. Ever since my dear wife died, they've been all I have in this world. Every moment I spend with them, I treasure in my heart."

"That's enough," Fargo said gruffly. "I get the idea." Rising, he scraped the bottom of his right boot on the log to remove a layer of mud clinging to the sole. If he had any sense at all, he told himself, he would refuse to take the Nuttalls another step. He would force them to turn around and head for Portland whether they wanted to or not. That was what he should do. Instead, he scowled up at the cloudy sky and said, "It must be all this rain. My brain is waterlogged."

"Meaning?" Nuttall asked hopefully.

"We go on," Fargo said, "but if you start to feel poorly, you're to tell me right away. And if you get too sick to ride, I'm putting my foot down. We'll rig a travois and head for the Columbia."

"A travois?"

As Fargo opened his mouth to detail how Indians hauled their effects on a platform crafted from long poles and buffalo rawhide, one of the pack animals started to act up. Snorting and plunging, it hauled on the lead rope, which Melissa held. She cried out as she was yanked forward and almost fell face first into the creek.

In several long bounds Fargo was there. Grabbing the rope, he dug in his heels and spoke softly to the horse to calm it. The animal kept glancing fearfully down at the water on either side of it. Fargo understood why when he saw a long, dark snake swimming upstream. He only caught a glimpse, not enough to identify whether it was poisonous or not.

The horse quieted. Fargo moved close to inspect its legs for fang marks. Thankfully, there were none, but as he straightened, he glanced at a strip of soft earth at the water's edge and saw something much worse than a snake.

Freshly made, no more than an hour old—if that—were a half-dozen clearly defined tracks.

Human tracks.

8

Skye Fargo pulled the packhorse onto the bank, then squatted beside the strip of bare, soggy ground for a closer look at the footprints. There had been two men. By comparing the size of their tracks to his own foot, he could tell that they were short in stature, a trait common among tribes living close to the coast. Why that should be, he didn't know. He also compared the depth of his print to theirs and found them to be about the same. Which indicated the warriors were stockily built, another common trait.

That was all Fargo could learn. He did change his guess on the time factor involved, cutting it from an hour to under thirty minutes. The Indians might still be in the area. They might even be spying on his party.

Without being obvious about it, Fargo scanned the surrounding forest as he strolled toward Davina. He was a few feet from her when he detected a flash of movement on the mountain that reared above the creek to the north. Low down, deep in the brush, a bronzed face was momentarily framed by branches and leaves. Then it disappeared.

Fargo casually draped his hand over the butt of his Colt. The redhead had stooped to splash water on her face and neck. As he came up beside her he said out of the corner of his mouth, "I'd hold off on a bath if I were you. There are Peeping Toms in the neighborhood."

Davina showed no alarm. She calmly unbent and ran a hand through her gorgeous locks. "How many, and where?"

Fargo told her, adding, "Don't let on that you know. Tell your sister and get ready to ride out." He drifted on around to the log where Nuttall was sketching again. "Has your heart been giving you any problems today?"

"Not at all," the painter said. "As a matter of fact, ever since we left San Francisco I've felt more fit than I have in ages."

"That's good to hear, because we have company," Fargo said. "Indians. I don't know if they're friendly, but we're not going to stick around to find out and maybe get an arrow in the back. Pack up all your pencils and paper and go climb on your horse."

In short order they were ready to go. Fargo idly tugged the big Henry from the boot and rested it across his thighs as he urged the Ovaro toward a shallow pool. He had started to enter the water when a warrior materialized as if out of thin air on the opposite bank. Reining up, Fargo announced without taking his eyes off the warrior, "Don't any of you lose your heads and do something we'll all regret. Smile and act real friendly and maybe we can get out of this without any trouble."

"What are you worried about? There are only two of them," Melissa said. "If they make any trouble, they're the ones who will be sorry."

"There are two that we know of," Fargo corrected her. "But for all we know, they might be with a large war party. Or their village could be near." His voice hardened. "So do as I tell you, damn it, or you'll answer to me later."

"Oh, my! I'm so scared!" Melissa teased.

The warrior had been studying them the whole time. He was not much more than five feet tall, but he was very broad of shoulder and chest. A small headdress made from fur and feathers crowned his oval head. It reminded Fargo of the style worn by the Karok Indians of northern California, as did the body armor that covered the warrior's torso and chin. Fashioned from hard rods bound tightly together, the armor could deflect arrows and knives.

But the man wasn't a Karok. Nor was he a Tlingit, though he had a large ring in his nose, as was Tlingit custom. His moccasins were more like high leather boots, similar to those favored by the Polatch tribe. His muscular forearms had tattoos on them, a Haida tradition. Slung across his back was a quiver full of arrows. In his right hand, held low at his side, was a short red bow.

"Do you know which tribe this fellow is from?" Nuttall inquired.

"Can't say as I do," Fargo said. "I'll try to find out." Resorting to sign language, he asked, "Question. You are called?" The man just stood there. His hands flowing smoothly, Fargo tried again. "Question. Your people are called?" But he might as well have been addressing a tree.

"Why doesn't he answer you?" Davina wanted to know.

"Few tribes in this neck of the woods are familiar with sign," Fargo disclosed. "But I had to try on the off chance he was." It worried him that the other warrior hadn't shown himself. Either the pair were merely distrustful of whites, or they were up to no good.

Suddenly the man on the bank gestured sharply and barked out words in a guttural tongue. Several times he jabbed a thick finger at the stallion and two of the pack animals.

"What is he blathering about?" Melissa asked. "Hasn't the idiot ever seen horses before?"

"I think he wants them."

"What?" Nuttall bleated.

"He's demanding three of our horses and most of our supplies," Fargo clarified. Shifting in the saddle, he said, "You're the leader of this expedition, Bill, so what you do with the packhorses is your business. But make no mistake. There is no way in hell I'm handing my pinto over to these two or anyone else. The only way they'll get him is if they pry the reins from my lifeless fingers."

Nuttall chewed on his lower lips. "I don't want to cause bloodshed, but we can't afford to lose a packhorse, can we?"

"No."

"Then I leave the decision in your capable hands. Whatever you say, we'll do."

Fargo nodded. "Get set, then. We might have to shoot our way out." Facing the warrior, he made a slashing gesture with his right arm and added a vigorous shake of his head for emphasis.

The man understood, all right. And he wasn't pleased. He repeated his demand, hefting his bow a few times as if threatening to use it if they did not do as he wanted.

Fargo already had a round in the Henry's chamber. Quietly thumbing back the hammer, he advanced into the creek, riding directly toward the warrior, who arrogantly held his ground until the stallion reached the bank on which he stood.

Lightning blazed in the man's dark eyes as he scowled and moved out of the way. He put his hand on the hilt of a long knife in a leather sheath on his right hip, but he did not draw it.

Fargo twisted. The Nuttalls were doing fine. Not one showed a trace of fear. Davina had a hand under her coat, while Melissa smirked at the warrior in blatant contempt. The last of the pack animals passed the Indian and he did nothing. Fargo glanced ahead, on the lookout for the other man. When he swung toward the creek again, the warrior on the bank was gone.

Intense itching broke out between Fargo's shoulder blades. At any moment his back might sprout a feathered shaft. The others were just as anxious but they hid their feelings well, except for their pinched expressions. He hoped the painter's heart would hold up under the strain.

When they had covered a hundred yards, Fargo paused. "From now on, always be on your guard. Never stray off. Never go into the bush alone."

Nuttall fidgeted. "Will they follow us, you think?"

"I'd lay money on it."

"To what end?"

"Your guess is as good as mine. If they're not out for blood, they might settle for plunder. Maybe they'll try to steal our horses. Or maybe they're partial to pretty females." Fargo let down the hammer on his rifle but kept the Henry in his lap. "As for you and me, we could wind up as slaves."

"Indians practice slavery? I never heard of such a thing."

"Some of the coast tribes do," Fargo revealed. "Take the Tlingits, for instance. They've been doing it for more years than any one of them can remember. Sometimes they trade for slaves with nearby tribes; sometimes they take them in war."

"White men, too?"

"Not the Tlingits. They like our trade goods too much, so they want us for friends. But there are others who have made slaves of trappers and sailors from time to time."

"Are the slaves well treated?"

Fargo glanced at him. "Does it matter? What man in his right mind wants to have others lord it over him?" He clucked to the stallion. "Keep this in mind. A slave has no say over whether he lives or dies." Fargo bent to go under a low limb. "Those Tlingits I mentioned like to throw a dead slave into the doorpost holes for every new house they build. It's supposed to bring them good medicine."

"My word!"

That ended the talk about slavery and put the three Nuttalls on their guard for the rest of the day. Fargo saw no sign of the warriors, but his every instinct told him they were always close by. If not for the painter's condition, he would have pushed on at a gallop and outdistanced them in no time. As it was, the best he could do was hold the horses to a trot when they came to flat terrain, which was not all that often. They were too deep in the mountains.

Well before dark, Fargo began searching for a sheltered spot to camp. He passed up a ravine because the walls were too steep. An opening at the base of a low cliff appeared promising from a distance but turned out to be barely high enough to sit in. The sun was perched on the peaks to the west when he rode up onto the crest of what he took for a ridge and discovered it as the rim of a wide, grassy basin. In the center stood an isolated knoll dotted with spruce trees.

"That will have to do," Fargo informed the others.

There was no spring. Not that they needed one. The rain had not let up once all day. Melissa set out several pots and soon had more water than they could use. Since Fargo insisted on a cold camp, their supper consisted of pemmican and venison jerky he had in his saddlebags.

Melissa turned up her nose at first but finally gave in to her hunger and nibbled on the pemmican. After she had swallowed, she grinned and said, "This isn't half-bad. Did you make it yourself? What's in it?"

"A Flathead woman gave me some on my way west," Fargo revealed. "Indians eat it all the time. They pound dried buffalo meat and mix it with crushed berries. Then they pour melted fat and marrow on top."

"Fat and marrow?" Melissa repeated, her distaste showing. She pried at a thin, circular layer under the fat. "But what's this? It almost looks like a membrane of some kind."

"It's part of the gut."

"The what?"

Fargo struggled to keep a straight face as he explained. "You'd call it the intestine. The paste is stuffed into a piece of buffalo gut, which is tied at both ends. Once the fat they coat it with hardens, the pemmican is done."

Melissa put a hand to her stomach. "Oh, Lord. I think I'm going to be sick."

Her father was chewing heartily. "Quit being such a baby, my dear. I don't care what's in it. The stuff is delicious. I only wish we'd had some with us on a few of our earlier expeditions when we were hard-pressed to find food."

Fargo took a bite of jerky. As he had talked, he watched the horses carefully for any sign that the warriors were near. So far the animals grazed contentedly. He had tied them to the trees rather than use the picket pins, and hobbled each one. The night was moonless and as black as pitch, perfect for would-be horse thieves.

The wind picked up, rustling the leaves and the grass. Fargo had draped his blanket over his head to protect his rifle from the rain, leaving it parted at the front so he could see out.

Over the next hour the four of them indulged in small talk. Fargo listened mostly, except when they plied him with questions about frontier life. Presently he declared, "It's time we were turning in. We're getting another early start tomorrow."

"I'll keep first watch," Davina volunteered.

Fargo had no objections. Odds were that if the warriors were going to try to make off with the horses, or anything else, they would make their move either before midnight, which would give them plenty of time to slip away in the dark and be long gone by daylight, or shortly before dawn, so they could race off once there was ample light to see. "Melissa can relieve you, and I'll relieve her," he proposed.

Nuttall was first under the blankets. For all his talk of being as fit as a fiddle, he fell asleep almost immediately. Melissa took longer, tossing and turning so much that Fargo began to wonder if she would ever doze off. At length she did. As for himself, he lay on his back, the Colt on his belly, the Henry at his side, and tried to relax enough to catch forty winks.

Davina wisely moved a few yards from the fire into a patch of shadow and wrapped herself in a blanket. She blended into the background so well that from just a few yards away she resembled a boulder or a tree stump.

It must have been close to one before slumber claimed Fargo. He did not sleep well. When Melissa took over for Davina, he woke up, even though they made as little noise as possible. When Nuttall got up in the middle of the night and went off behind a tree, he woke up again. Try as he might, he couldn't slip back into dreamland until half an hour after the artist resumed sawing logs.

When a hand fell lightly on his shoulder, Fargo shot up, leveling the Colt. He felt sheepish when he saw who it was.

Melissa jerked back and whispered, "I know we don't get along very well, but I didn't think you'd blow my brains out just because you don't like me."

Fargo was drowsy from lack of sleep or he would never have said what he did. "You're putting words in my mouth. A man would have to be a few cards shy of a full deck not to admire a fine-looking woman like you."

"Oh?" Melissa said, and somehow made her bosom swell to twice its normal size. Smiling seductively, she patted her hair. "You certainly hide your feelings well. I would never have guessed you were fond of me."

Wisps of fatigue evaporated as Fargo gave his head a toss, and stood. "Go ahead and turn in. You'll need all the rest you can get." Holstering the Colt, he pulled the green blanket close about him and sat in the spot Davina had occupied earlier. The rifle's stock went on the ground between his legs so he could prop it up without using his hands.

The air was cooler, the wind brisker. A chorus of howls and yips were proof the creatures of the night were abroad. Fargo tilted the Henry against his shoulder and counted the horses to be sure all seven were there.

It was hard staying awake. His fatigue conspired with the whispering sigh of the wind to render his mind blank and turn his limbs to mush. He dozed, but instantly snapped his head upright again. Resolved to stay awake at all costs, Fargo stood back up and paced, stamping his boots to get his blood pumping. He walked over to the dozing stallion and scratched behind its ears.

As he stood there between the pinto and a bay, a sorrel to the east pricked its ears and snorted. Instantly Fargo crouched and let the blanket slide off to free his arms. A light drizzle fell, the patter of drops muffling any noise the sorrel might have heard.

How long Fargo held himself still, he couldn't say. His patience was rewarded when something moved off in the darkness. Whatever it was, it hugged the ground, as a crawling man would do.

The figure froze when William Nuttall shifted and muttered in his sleep. When convinced it was safe, the warrior came closer. He would move a foot or so, then freeze. Move another foot, and freeze again.

Fargo had been holding the Henry with the barrel angled down. He had to raise the gun to shoot, but he had to raise it without drawing attention to himself—or the warrior would be gone like a shot. So every time the warrior moved, he did also, hiking the Henry toward his shoulder, then pausing when the Indian did the same.

One thing bothered him. Where was the second man? Fargo swiveled his eyes from side to side yet saw no one else. Unexpectedly, the sorrel took a few steps, blundering into his line of fire. He couldn't see the warrior. Quickly he tucked the stock to his shoulder and silently moved forward a few feet.

The sorrel nervously retraced its steps. Fargo thought he had the warrior dead to rights, but he was in for a nasty surprise. The warrior was gone! His eyes raked the slope from top to bottom, but he didn't see anyone.

Had the man spotted him? Fargo pivoted to the right and the left but no one was sneaking up on him. Then a bush ten feet away unfurled and took on the shape of a squatting man. Fargo went to take a bead. As he did, the Ovaro nickered, and a fraction of a second later the pad-pad-pad of rushing feet made Fargo aware of the blunder he had committed.

The warrior in front of him served as a *diversion*. The real threat was bearing down from the rear.

Fargo whirled at the very moment that a burly form sprang. A stout war club struck the Henry, jarring the rifle from Fargo's grasp a heartbeat before the warrior's body smashed into his, bowling him over. He landed on his back and slid under the sorrel, which saved him from a second swing of the club but put him in peril of being stomped to death as the frightened horse pranced and kicked.

Shielding his head with his arms, Fargo rolled out from under the animal. A hoof clipped him on the shoulder but not hard enough to break the bone. He barely saw the warrior pounce in time. As he flipped onto his side the war club struck the exact spot where his head had been.

Lashing out with his right leg, Fargo caught the warrior in the leg. The man tottered, snarled, and arced the club at his face. Fargo dodged with a whisker to spare. At the same time he grabbed for his Colt, cocked it as he cleared leather, and fired as the warrior threw himself past the sorrel. A grunt proved he had scored but he must have missed a vital organ because the warrior bounded off into the darkness with all the speed and agility of an antelope. So did his companion.

Shouts from the Nuttalls laced the night as Fargo slowly rose. Lady Luck had saved his hide, nothing else. Disgusted at himself for making a blunder typical of a raw greenhorn, he replaced the spent cartridge. The artist and the women dashed over as he snatched up the Henry. They all started talking at once. He silenced them by lifting his hand. Removing his red bandanna, he started to wipe the rifle off.

"Well, are you going to tell us what happened?" Melissa demanded. "What was the shooting about?"

"Our friends paid us a visit," was all Fargo would say. "They got away, but I don't think they'll bother us for a while. One of them is wounded."

"Were they after the horses,?" Nuttall asked.

"No," Fargo said, and let it go at that. "Why don't all of you turn back in? It's still a couple of hours until dawn. No need to waste them."

"I doubt I could sleep after this," Melissa said. "If you'll give me permission to get a small fire going, I'll fix coffee and biscuits."

Fargo saw no harm in having a fire now. "Go ahead. I'll be there in a minute."

The black-haired beauty and her father walked off. Not the redhead. Davina fixed him with a knowing look and said bluntly, "We're in a hell of a fix, aren't we? You scared them off, but they're bound to be back, and the next time they'll bring friends along. Lots of friends."

"That's how I figure it," Fargo agreed. "So you tell me. Do we throw your father over his horse and ride like the wind for the Columbia or do we see this thing through? I know what I'd do, but he's your father so you can decide."

"Thanks for nothing," Davina said, with no bitterness. She slid the pistol in her hand into a holster while watching her father and sister gathering wood. "My head tells me to do one thing and my heart another. I love him, Skye, and I don't want him to come to harm. But this is his last expedition, his last bird. It would crush him if we gave up. I say we go on."

Fargo finished drying off the Henry. He found the blanket he had dropped and walked to where Melissa, huddled under a tree, was coaxing a few fairly dry twigs into flame. It took some doing, but the fire caught.

As William and Davina gathered around, Fargo leaned against the trunk. Off in the distance an owl hooted, and for some odd reason he thought of the many birds they had seen on their trek. Ospreys and swallows along the river, meadowlarks and sparrows in the meadows, robins and chickadees in the woods, and eagles and hawks higher up. It brought to mind a question he asked the artist. "Where exactly is the best place to find this blue tanager of yours?"

"I told you. Mount Saint Helens," Nuttall said.

"Where, though? In the forests around it? In nearby meadows? Or along streams in the area?"

"Oh. I see what you mean." Nuttall held his hands out to the fire to warm them. "No, the blue tanager nests on the slope of the mountain itself. We'll have to climb Mount Saint Helens."

"But it's a volcano. And it likes to erupt every now and then."

"I know." The painter grinned. "That's what makes our adventure so exciting."

Fargo looked up through the branches at the shroud of clouds and half wished a bolt of lightning would strike him and put him out of his misery. He made himself a promise. If he was ever in jail again and a stranger offered to bail him out, he'd strangle the son of a bitch.

The new day dawned dreary and cold. Instead of a blazing sun they were treated to renewed rain, prompting Melissa Nuttall to complain at one point, "Doesn't it ever stop? I swear, Washington must be a salamander's idea of heaven."

They seldom spoke. Even the painter, when they spotted birds, had nothing to say. They were tired and on edge. Just how on edge became apparent a few hours after sunrise. Davina was in charge of the pack animals, and when one of them balked at climbing a talus slope, she lashed it with a rope and swore as lustily as a seaman.

It was a rare outburst for her and showed Fargo that he had to keep an eye on his charges to see that their frazzled nerves did not result in serious mistakes. When Melissa began to doze in the saddle toward the middle of the morning, he rode back and shook her, saying, "No sleeping until tonight. I don't want you falling off and hitting your head on a rock."

True to her nature, she snickered and responded, "Why, Mr. Fargo, how sweet of you to fret about my being hurt."

"I doubt it would hurt all that much," Fargo retorted. "As hard as your head is, the rock would probably break." He rode to the front of the line before she could take a swing at him.

Twice before noon Fargo let the Nuttalls ride on ahead while he looped around to the south to see if they were being shadowed. There was no sign of the warriors. Fargo hoped that would be the end of it, but he had gone up against Indians too many times to believe that the pair had given up.

Many whites back in the States liked to brand all Indians as cowardly devils who only attacked when they had the advantage. Newspaper reporters were always going on about the "yellow heathens" who made life miserable for "brave whites everywhere." But as with so much the press wrote, it simply wasn't so.

Fargo had lived with Indians. The Sioux, the Shoshones, the Flatheads, he knew them all well. He had learned that although Indian and white customs were so different, when all was said and done, the two peoples had more in common that either would admit. He had also learned that warriors were as brave as any white, and never to be taken lightly.

So even though the whole day went by without Fargo catching a glimpse of the two men, he did not relax his guard.

By evening they were all worn out. The terrain had been the roughest yet, and when they drew rein in a clearing on a shelf halfway up a mountain, all the horses hung their heads in exhaustion. Including the Ovaro.

A creek meandered over the shelf at the west end. Fargo led the horses to a small pool and made sure they did not drink too much. Unlike mules, which had the good sense never to drink themselves sick, thirsty horses would guzzle until they were bloated. He had to stop a pack animal insistent on making itself so ill it would be useless the next day.

Fargo allowed Davina to make a small fire in a depression close to the side of the mountain. The Nuttalls had to erect a lean-to first to keep out the rain, and finding enough dry wood to last took hours.

Since they had not had a hot supper the day before, Fargo went hunting as twilight cloaked the forest. He could go another week, or as long as need be, on jerky and pemmican, but the others were not hardened to wilderness life as he was. A hot meal would do wonders for their constitutions and their spirits. Just before it became almost too dark to see, a plump raccoon blundered across his path. The coon saw him and bounded toward a thicket. He had the Henry in his left hand at the time so he resorted to the Colt, drawing and snapping off a single shot.

As Fargo carried his prize into camp, Melissa contorted her pretty face and said, "Surely you don't expect me to eat *that?*

We're not from the South, you know. We don't eat opossum, either."

"Suit yourself," Fargo said. "The pemmican is in my saddle-bags."

"I had quite enough of that, thank you."

But once Fargo had butchered the coon and was roasting juicy chunks over the crackling flames, Melissa drew near and sat with her arms wrapped around her knees, eyeing the meat as if she were a starved panther about to pounce on prey. She licked her lips when Fargo tested a piece and made a show of smacking his mouth to show how tasty it was. When he pulled the first morsel off the trimmed branch, she was right there, asking for it.

William Nuttall was strangely quiet during the meal. Once Fargo caught the older man studying him, and when the artist realized it, Nuttall glanced away and seemed embarrassed. Later, after everyone was done, Nuttall stepped to a flat boulder and sat on it to smoke his pipe.

A cup of hot coffee in hand, Fargo walked over. He had the feeling that the man had something on his mind, and he was right. But the question Nuttall posed was the last one he expected to hear.

"I've heard you say more than once that you're not the marrying kind. Is that etched in stone?"

"Any reason it shouldn't be?"

Nuttall stared at his daughters. "Melissa. You handle her better than any man ever has. At long last she's met her match. I think the two of you would make a fine pair." He sighed. "It's my fondest wish, Skye, that before I die both my girls will tie the knot. They would have married long ago if I wasn't always dragging them from one end of the country to the other. They hardly get to know a man before they're gallivanting off somewhere else."

"Don't be so hard on yourself. I've noticed that when a woman is ready to marry, nothing will hold her back. Your daughters just aren't ready yet."

"I'd like to believe that. I truly would. But I fear the blame is all mine."

Fargo downed some of his coffee. The painter looked to be on the verge of tears, so he said, "You should be proud of yourself. You've raised a pair of strong-willed women who can hold their own against anyone, anywhere. I've met a lot of females in my travels but few were as tough as your two."

Nuttall brightened. "You really think so?"

"I know so." Fargo gave the man a friendly pat on the back and ambled to the horses. Since few trees grew on the shelf, he had tethered them to picket pins, which he now checked to insure none had worked loose. It wouldn't do to have any of the animals stray off in the middle of the night.

Taking a seat on a little grassy bump on the far side of the string, Fargo sipped the rest of his Arbuckle's while gazing out over the forested landscape they had covered that day. No telltale pinpoints of light flickered in the night. If the two Indians were still back there, they'd had the presence of mind to conceal their campfire.

It was quiet and peaceful there in the darkness. Fargo lingered, losing all track of time. He nursed his cup as long as he could. As he rose to go turn in, a shadow came toward him. He had seen Nuttall crawl under the covers a while ago. Now he noticed that one of the women had a blanket hiked clear up over her head. Davina was supposed to stand guard first, so he greeted the shadow by that name.

"Wrong guess, dummy," Melissa said, coming close enough for him to see her lovely face. "I asked sis to switch and she agreed. Hope you don't mind."

"It doesn't matter," Fargo said to avoid an argument.

Melissa had a rifle with her. She held it in the crook of her left elbow and tilted her head back to look at the clouds. In doing so her chest swelled, her large breasts straining against the soft wool shirt she wore under her jacket. "Thank God the rain has almost stopped. Any day now I expect to find moss growing out of my ears."

"They say that's how you can always tell a person from Washington Territory," Fargo said. "That, and the ferns growing between their toes."

Light laughter rose from the throat of the woman who had

100

treated him as if he were beneath contempt since the day they met. Fargo looked down at his boots so she wouldn't see his grin. His loins twitched in anticipation.

Melissa coughed. "I could use some exercise. Would it hurt if the two of us went for a short stroll?"

Fargo was not about to let her off the hook so easily. "I suppose it wouldn't, if we keep the camp in sight." He let her take a stride, then said, "But I'm a bit surprised that a prissy woman like you would want to be alone with a barbarian like me."

"Prissy?" Melissa grated between her perfect teeth.

"What was it you called me back in San Francisco? A Goth, as I recollect," Fargo baited her. "I don't know exactly what that is, but I know an insult when I hear one. You must get cross-eyed a lot from going around looking down your nose at everyone."

"Now see here—" Melissa began.

"Don't be upset," Fargo said politely. "You can't help it if you're a bitch. Some people are just born that way."

The black-haired firebrand exploded. Hissing like a mad cat, she swept her right hand up to slap him.

Fargo was ready. He caught her wrist and twisted her arm— not hard, but hard enough to make her gasp. She tried to tug free, and when that failed, she let go of her rifle and clawed at his eyes with her left hand. Slapping it aside, he applied more leverage to her arm and gave her a shove. Melissa stumbled a step, then whirled, her fists clenched, her dander up.

"How dare you, you bastard! You have the manners of a drunken lout! Do you know what I'd like to do to you?"

"This," Fargo said, and stepped close to glue his body to hers. His mouth descended to her soft lips as his right hand closed on her full breast and his left pressed at the junction of her shapely thighs. She stiffened, pushed him back, and huffed in outrage.

"I'll shoot you for this! No man takes liberties with me and gets away with it!"

"I wasn't taking liberties," Fargo said, moving up to her again. "I was doing what you wanted me to do." Curling an

101

arm around her slender waist, he kissed her passionately, his hands roving up and down her exquisite form. She quivered a moment, snapped her head away, and raised her hand to strike him.

"Go right ahead, if that will make you happy," Fargo said, "but we both know this is what you really want." He locked his lips on hers a third time. She went rigid, batting at his shoulders. For a moment he thought he was wrong. But her blows were light, and after only a few she rested her hands on his chest and clutched at his shirt as if she were afraid of falling. Her mouth parted to admit his tongue.

Melissa Nuttall was a temperamental woman. Her moods swung in extremes. One moment she could be as cold as ice, the next as hot as an inferno. She demonstrated that now by roaming her hands over his chest, his back, his buttocks. She delighted him by boldly reaching for his manhood and stroking his hard pole from bottom to top. Her agile tongue probed his mouth.

Fargo glanced over a shoulder. Her father and sister both appeared to be asleep, but Davina's blanket had slipped down to her ears. Cupping Melissa's trim bottom, he hefted her off the ground and carried her deeper into the darkness. She nibbled on his neck, his ears, his chin. When he set her down, she wrapped her left leg around him and tugged at his shirt. He did likewise and slipped a hand up underneath. To his surprise, she wore no underclothes. He felt smooth skin under his palm, skin that rippled and erupted in goosebumps when he slid his calloused hand up over her ribs to her ripe mounds. His fingers pinched a hardening nipple and gave its twin the same attention.

"Oh, God," Melissa breathed, quivering with the intensity of her long-suppressed desire.

Fargo massaged both breasts, feeling them grow warmer and warmer, as did her breath on his neck and her lips on his flesh. She could not seem to get enough of him. Her mouth, her hands, her whole body were in constant motion. Hiking her shirt high enough to expose her nipples, he fastened his mouth to first one and then the other. She wriggled and made low gurgling sounds, her fingers entwined in his hair.

Melissa was making so much noise that Fargo lifted her again and carried her farther from the fire. Whether William Nuttall approved of him or not, he didn't feel comfortable making love to the man's daughter with the artist so close. They came to the creek, to a red cedar. Fargo backed her against the trunk and dropped his hands to her thighs. She had been wearing pants ever since they left the Columbia, tight pants that bulged in all the right places, pants so tight that when Fargo ran his hands between her legs he could feel the heat of her womanhood and spreading dampness.

Melissa arched her spine at that first contact, her long fingernails digging tiny furrows in his shoulders. When she kissed him next, her lips were aflame, her skin molten with desire. She whined deep in her throat and shoved her hips against him to stroke his passion.

Fargo was not worried about the Indians coming on them. With one warrior wounded, it was doubtful the pair had been able to keep up with the horses. Either they were somewhere back along the trail or they had gone to their village for more men. In any event, it would be a day or two before they made more trouble. He could relax and enjoy himself.

Slipping his lips over the end of her hard right nipple, Fargo sucked and licked, flicking the tip with his tongue. He squeezed her other globe, kneading it until the breast swelled and she squirmed with each tweak. Easing upward, he lathered her throat, then sucked on an earlobe. She was sensitive there, and his warm breath on her ear made her gyrate her hips. Her hand fumbled inside his pants, encircled his organ, and lightly stroked.

For all her sensual hunger, Melissa was gentle with him, far more so than her sister had been. Davina wrestled a man down and went at him like a she-cat in the grip of unbridled lust; Melissa let the man take control but matched his ardor with her own. Given their dispositions, he would have thought it would be the other way around. But that was the marvelous thing about women. They were never predictable.

Fargo traced a path with his tongue from a throbbing vein in her throat, down between her twin peaks, to her navel. He swirled it around, causing her to shiver. When he lowered his mouth to the top of her pants, he felt her belly ripple under him. Unhooking her store-bought britches, he pulled them down to her knees and did the same with her underpants. A tantalizing dank fragrance made his mouth water.

At the first touch of his mouth to her nether lips, Melissa moaned and sank to the ground. He eased down as she did, never breaking contact. Spreading her legs wide and hooking them over his shoulders, he bored into her like a badger boring into a burrow. She grasped his head to shove him in deeper, her eyes shut, her rosy lips parted in ecstasy. As her fervor mounted she clamped her thighs against the sides of his head, as if afraid he would try to pull back before she wanted him to.

Fargo had no such intention. He knew women too well, knew that some took a lot of time to reach the pinnacle of release. Patience was the key. Too many men made love as if it were a despised duty they had to finish as soon as possible. Not him. Fargo always took his sweet time, matching his pace to the woman's. Her satisfaction was just as important as his. Because, as he'd learned long ago, satisfy a woman once and odds were that she would come back for a second helping.

Melissa humped herself into him while twisting his hair clear down to the roots. She slipped a hand under his shirt and raked his back, drawing blood. When he raised his head to kiss her, she lowered her legs to his midriff and locked them around his waist.

Fargo sank his hand to the entrance to her moist cave. His middle finger slipped inside. She bucked a few times, her slick inner walls closing around him like a sheath. He added another finger, then pumped them. Melissa fastened her mouth to his neck and sucked as if trying to draw blood.

To their right was a patch of grass. Slowly easing Melissa onto her back, Fargo stretched out and dropped his pants. His pole jutted at her like a war lance. She ran her fingertips its entire length, cupped his jewels, and extended a finger between his legs. The sensation sent a tingle rippling up his spine to the base of his skull.

Cupping her mound, Fargo rubbed her core. She tossed her head, mewing like a kitten. He ran his mouth up along her side from her stomach to under her arm. Her breasts were taut, her nipples erect. Covering one with his free hand, he placed his mouth on hers and sucked her tongue into his mouth as if it were a piece of hard candy. She returned the favor, her hands tugging at his hips.

Fargo eased between her legs. Melissa knew just what to do and elevated her backside. With a sharp thrust, he penetrated her to the hilt. It took her by surprise and she cried out, but softly. To forestall more cries she bit her lower lip. He held her by the thighs, balanced on his knees, then began thrusting into her over and over. She was soft and warm and yielding, everything a woman should be and more, her craving the equal of his. Soon she was matching his rhythm, and in unison they climbed toward the summit of carnal pleasure.

For a brief span Fargo forgot about the Indians and the volcano and the blue tanager and everything else except the ravishing woman under him. Their mouths were fused, their tongues creating enough friction to set kindling on fire. Her hands were everywhere; his held her firmly so she wouldn't slide out from under him on the damp grass. Faster and faster they went, until, all of a sudden, Melissa Nuttall stiffened, the whites of her eyes showing as she passed the brink. She went crazy, her limbs flying, her body trying to heave up off the ground. It was all Fargo could do to hold on, but he did, and when she gushed, so did he, penetrating her to the depths of her being.

Much later they lay on their backs, Melissa's head resting on the big man's shoulder. She contentedly ran a finger back and forth across his chest while her toes played with his leg. Fargo wanted to doze off but he couldn't. He had one more thing to do before he turned in.

"Not bad for a barbarian," Melissa teased.

"Not bad for a prissy bitch," Fargo retorted, and was poked

in the ribs so hard that it was a miracle none cracked. It had not taken long for things to get back to normal.

The brisk breeze inspired Melissa to sit up and dress. Fargo followed her example. A check of the fire showed her father and sister were both asleep and most of the horses were dozing.

Melissa stood on tiptoe to peck his cheek. "You're a special man, even if you do have rocks between your ears," she whispered. "Too bad you're not in the market or I'd latch onto you and never let go." She caressed his jaw rather wistfully, then spun and hurried off, her head bowed, stopping along the way to pick up her rifle.

Fargo adjusted his gun belt and made sure no moisture had gotten on the Colt. His ankle sheath had slipped down so he retied the thin leather strap. Pulling his hat brim low, he ambled back. The dull glint of tin reminded him of the coffee cup he had dropped.

Melissa was pouring herself a cup when he got there. She held the pot out and he helped himself. They looked at one another, her eyes smoldering with a longing he could never satisfy, as they both well knew.

"What will you do when our expedition is over with?" Melissa asked.

The Trailsman shrugged. "Maybe ride east. Follow the Columbia into Nez Percé country, and from there go visit the Shoshones. I did a chief of theirs a favor a while back, and every time I stop by he goes out of his way to make me feel at home."

"I envy you, the freedom you have, the places you've seen, but I'm glad this is the last time out for my father. To tell the truth, I'm tired of all our wandering. I'd like to find myself a fellow who thinks I'm God's gift to men and settle down to raise a family." Melissa sniffed. "Never thought I would hear myself say that. When I was younger, I expected to be a spinster all my life."

Fargo raised his cup. The wind was in his face, and as he went to drink he smelled a stench so foul that his stomach churned. He covered is nose and mouth with a hand and saw

Melissa imitating him. At the same instant, a twig snapped loudly in the forest beyond the creek.

Leaping erect, Fargo exchanged the cup for the Henry. The stench was gone as mysteriously as it had appeared, and he inhaled deeply to clear out his lungs. Suddenly all of the horses were upright, their ears pricked. Not one let out a peep, as if they were too scared to make a noise.

"What is it?" Melissa whispered. "A skunk? A bear?"

Fargo shook his head. That awful odor had been unlike any polecat or bear scent he knew. Taking a few steps, he peered long and hard into the night. Once again he felt as if he were being watched, but he saw nothing. The stench returned, more powerful, more nauseating than before. It reminded him of a maggot-infested buffalo carcass long baked by a hot sun. Only worse.

William Nuttall sputtered in his sleep and rolled over to put his back to the breeze.

Davina coughed, then sat up and looked around in confusion. When she saw Fargo with his rifle poised, she was on her feet in a flash, her two pistols out and cocked. "What's going on?" she asked. "What's out there?"

Before Fargo could answer, all hell broke loose.

10

A tremendous roar ripped the night, a roar so loud that it sounded as if three grizzlies were voicing their collective fury at the same time. It was a roar unlike any Fargo had ever heard, more feral than any wolf's, more piercing than any mountain lion's, more menacing than any wolverine's. It made the short hairs at the nape of his neck prickle, his pulse pound. He sighted down the Henry, but there was no target to shoot at. A black veil shrouded the woods, and within it nothing moved.

The same could not be said of the horses. At the hideous roar, they burst into panic. All of them were whinnying and tugging at their picket pins. Several reared, or tried to, and were drawn up short by the picket ropes. The animal nearest the creek, a sorrel, went into a frenzy, bucking and tossing its head in wild abandon.

"We can't let any of them get loose!" Davina cried, running to quiet them.

"Wait!" Fargo responded, afraid that whatever lurked out there would rush out of the dark and be on her before he could squeeze off a shot. She paid him no mind, so he jogged after her as another blistering roar seemed to shake the very ground. The terrible stink enveloped him, more nauseating than any foul odor had any right to be. He could barely stand to breathe.

Across the creek rose a riotous breaking of limbs and rending of brush. It sounded as if large branches were being crunched in half and whole bushes torn out by the roots and flung about.

Davina was almost to the horses. Suddenly the sorrel reared

backward. Its picket pin came out and the horse immediately whirled and fled from the terror in the trees. In its blind fear, the sorrel thundered down the middle of the shelf, straight toward the redhead.

"Look out!" Fargo shouted.

Davina flapped her arms and hollered in an attempt to stop the animal, but it had no effect. Eyes wide, ears laid back, tail erect, the sorrel bore down on her like a runaway steam engine, its heavy hooves churning the earth and sending large clods of dirt flying. She tensed on the balls of her feet. Just when it appeared certain that she would be trampled, she leaped clear.

A dozen feet behind her, Fargo abruptly found himself directly in the path of the onrushing animal. He sprang to the side, but as he did his left foot slipped on the grass. His leg swept out from under him, pitching him onto his knees. The sorrel was almost on him. Glancing up, he saw its muscular legs swiftly pounding closer. There was no time to hurl himself out of the way, so he did the only thing he could. Fargo threw himself flat, covered the back of his head with his arms, and yelled.

Thunder boomed in his ears. Clumps of dirt rained down on him. Out of the corner of an eye he saw the sorrel's flying hooves smash onto the earth less than a yard from his face. He braced for the bone-splitting impact to come. And then the hooves flew skyward, sailing up and over his body. The horse had vaulted over him, as it would a log or low boulder. He heard rather than saw it crash down. Twisting, he was just in time to see it streak between William Nuttall and Melissa and race on into the night. The rope trailed beside it, the picket pin bumping and bouncing like a deranged jackrabbit.

The rest of the horses were still beside themselves with fright, with one notable exception. Standing silently among them was the pinto stallion, its flanks quivering, its gaze on the forest.

So was Fargo's. The rending of vegetation had ceased and been replaced by an eerie stillness. He stood as Nuttall and Melissa hastened to help Davina with the horses. Melissa paused to ask if he was all right. Fargo nodded, his head cocked. He covered the Nuttalls while they calmed the horses, then advised them to hobble every last one, except the Ovaro.

The woods was still. Fargo no longer had the feeling that he was being watched. Whatever had been out there must have been enormous, yet it had crept off as quietly as a tiny mouse. It might have been a grizzly, he told himself, since the fierce silvertips could be virtual ghosts when they wanted to be.

A year or so earlier, Fargo had been washing his coffeepot in a high-country lake in the northern Rockies when he had turned around to find a massive grizzly not ten feet away. The brute had snuck up on him without disturbing so much as a pebble. Thankfully, its belly had been full or it would have torn into him before he could get off a shot. It had sniffed a few times, snorted as if it did not like his scent, and melted into the forest without making a sound.

The Nuttalls clustered around the fire. Since the fleeing packhorse had knocked over the coffeepot, Melissa set about making a fresh batch. Fargo escorted her to the creek for water, and as they backed away she turned to him.

"What the hell was that thing? One of those creatures you told us about? A Skoo-kum, I think you called it?"

Fargo had almost forgotten about the Klikitat belief. In all his travels he had never come across any such creature, so he had not taken their claim all that seriously. Yet many tribes believed in things like lake monsters and mysterious beasts that prowled the deep woods, creatures few had ever seen. "I don't know," he admitted, adding lamely, "It could have been just a bear."

"A bear with a temper. Let's hope it doesn't come back."

William Nuttall had a different worry on his mind. "What are we going to do about the sorrel?" he asked as they approached. "We can't simply go off and leave it. I doubt it would last very long on its own, what with all the big cats and other predators about."

Fargo hunkered down to warm himself. "I'll go after it at first light," he suggested. "The three of you pack up and be ready to ride when I get back."

"Maybe one of us should go along," Davina proposed.

"I can travel faster by my lonesome," Fargo said. None of them could ride as well as he could. And he needed the redhead to stay behind to protect her father and sister. "If all goes well, I won't be long. The sorrel shouldn't have gone far."

But the horse proved the big man wrong. A pale, rosy glow tinted the cloud cover to the east when Fargo jabbed his heels into the stallion and trotted into the pines. Here in the trees the shadows were long and dark, so he held the Henry with the stock propped on his thigh. It was not hard to track the packhorse. For the first mile it had smashed through the undergrowth like an elk in rut run amok. After that, tired from its flight, it had moved along at a brisk walk, sticking to open ground.

Fargo's hope was that the animal had stopped after a while and bedded down for the rest of the night. Any horse with any sense would have done so, but the troublesome sorrel had gone on and on. By the middle of the morning Fargo knew that he would never overtake it before noon. So he had a decision to make. Should he give up and go back, or keep on no matter how long it took? They could get by with the two packhorses left. But Nuttall was bound to be upset at the loss, and it was best not to let anything worsen the artist's delicate condition. So Fargo continued eastward.

Midday brought him to yet another stream. The countryside was laced with them, a result of the heavy rainfall the region received. He located a clearing where the sorrel had grazed for a short while before going on.

For the life of him, Fargo could not figure out why the animal was in such a hurry. It was in the middle of nowhere, heading nowhere fast.

About two in the afternoon, Fargo crested a barren spine. Hoofprints wound down through sparse timber to a verdant valley. He started to descend but hauled on the reins when he spied other tracks paralleling those of the sorrel. The new prints displayed four toes arranged in a curved row and a large heel pad. Each was over four and a half inches wide. There

111

was no evidence of claw marks, as there would be if a wolf or coyote had made the prints.

Fargo's mouth tightened into a slit. The tracks were those of a mountain lion, or cougar, as trappers in the Northwest liked to call the big cats. And this one had been quite big—larger than most, judging by the size of the prints. Shifting, he noticed that the cougar had emerged from a cluster of boulders at the top. It had been lying up there, waiting for a deer or other prey to come along, when the sorrel had blundered onto the scene.

Slapping his legs, Fargo went down the slope on the fly. The cat's tracks stayed close to the pack animal's until near the bottom. There, the feline had closed in. Fargo doubted the sorrel had had any inkling it was being stalked until the mountain lion pounced. A puddle of blood marked the exact spot.

Cougars preferred to jump prey from behind, fasten their razor teeth into the neck or spine of their victim, then rake and slash with their long claws until the animal dropped from shock or loss of blood.

Evidently the sorrel had put up a struggle. A broken bush showed where the mountain lion had been bucked off. It had scrambled erect and a chase had ensued. The horse had made off across the valley with the cat at its heels.

Fargo had seen mountain lions go after deer, and he knew that if they missed their first spring, they had to catch their quarry quickly. The big cats were incredibly powerful but they lacked endurance. If they couldn't bring their prey down within a hundred yards or so, they grew winded and gave up.

In his mind's eye, Fargo pictured the terrified sorrel fleeing for its life while the cougar clawed at its hind legs. If it had faltered or tripped, the cat would have leaped onto its flanks. That was exactly what must have happened, because he came on a wide trail of blood that had not yet had time to dry.

The grass was so high that Fargo could not see for more than thirty feet. Ahead was trampled grass smeared with more blood. He rose in the stirrups for a better look, and instantly halted.

In a glistening scarlet pool lay the sorrel. One leg was

twisted at an unnatural angle, the bone poking through the ruptured skin. Astride the horse's belly was the deadly cat. Its claws were hooked into the sorrel's flesh. Blood caked its chin and whiskers. The mountain lion had heard the Ovaro coming and was looking right at Fargo. An ominous snarl warned him that if he came any closer, the cat would defend its kill.

Fargo raised the Henry, then just as promptly lowered it. He could not blame the cougar for doing what came naturally. In the scheme of things, the big cats culled the deer and elk herds by eliminating the weak and the sick. It was the sorrel's misfortune to have taken the place of the lion's natural quarry that day.

Without delay, Fargo trotted westward. The cougar made no attempt to follow. Skye squinted up at the high sun and realized it would be impossible to rejoin the Nuttalls before nightfall. He trusted that they had not strayed off, and would have a fire going when he got there. But eventually he came within sight of the mountain, and no light was visible.

Through a dark forest gone uncommonly quiet, Fargo ascended the slope below the shelf. He yanked the Henry from the saddle scabbard, dreading the sight that would greet him.

The artist and his daughters were gone. So were the horses. Broken, smashed, and discarded supplies had been scattered every which way, among them a busted paintbrush near the dead fire. Fargo dismounted and lowered a hand to the embers. A few were still warm. Whatever had happened had taken place within the past three or four hours.

His first priority was to get the fire going again. A burning brand raised on high, Fargo roamed the shelf seeking clues. There were no claw marks on any of the littered provisions. But there were moccasin tracks all over the place. Fargo's best guess was that fifteen warriors had been in the war party. They had converged from four directions, taking the Nuttalls unaware. Or had they?

Over by the creek the grass was dotted with drops of blood. Crushed blades and scuff marks indicated that one of the three had put up a hell of a fight. Fargo circled the shelf to learn which way the war party had gone with their captives. To his surprise, it was due north, toward the unexplored region around Mount Saint Helens.

"Damn," Fargo said as he straightened. He had his work cut out for him. Hurrying to the fire, he stamped it out, extinguished the brand, and forked leather. Even though he endangered the stallion by traveling at night, he had no choice. Every mile the war party gained on him increased the likelihood that he would catch up with them too late to save the Nuttalls, if in fact the Indians planned to do them harm. Squaring his shoulders, he headed out.

For once no rain fell. A break in the clouds allowed Fargo his first glimpse of the sky in days. He slid the rifle back into the boot, since if it fell from his hands he would have a hard time finding it in the dark. He couldn't afford a single delay.

The Ovaro was tired, but the big stallion trotted smoothly along. One of the reasons Fargo refused to part with the pinto was its superb stamina. It could cover twice as much ground as any ordinary mount before fatigue set in.

Fargo tested the air often. Whatever had paid their camp a visit the night before was bound to be abroad again, and he would rather spot the thing before it spotted him.

Few Indians liked to travel at night. And among some tribes, warfare itself was conducted only during daylight hours. So Fargo was optimistic that the war party had already bedded down, and if all went well he would reach their camp before midnight. But that hour came and went and he still had not spotted a campfire.

Reluctantly, Fargo reined up. It was possible the Indians had changed direction and he had lost their trail altogether, in which case he would have to spend hours the next morning hunting for it again. He stripped off his saddle and bedroll and sat with his back to a pine, a blanket over his shoulders. As tired as he was, he couldn't sleep. His mind was racing too fast. He was worried that the warriors had something else in mind besides making the Nuttalls slaves. Some tribes indulged in torture and liked to prolong the suffering of their captives as long as they could. William Nuttall wouldn't last five minutes.

It was two hours before sunrise when Fargo at last succumbed to slumber, and it seemed as if he had hardly closed his eyes when the chirping of sparrows awakened him to a light drizzle. He wasted no time in saddling up and mounting. His breakfast was jerky, eaten on the go.

As it turned out, Fargo had not lost the trail after all. The war party simply had not halted for the night. For men on foot they were making remarkable time. He spurred the Ovaro to a canter and held that pace as frequently as the terrain permitted.

All the while, Fargo grew steadily closer to Mount Saint Helens. Up close, cloaked in the gloom of rain and clouds, the volcano was a foreboding sight. Rearing close to ten thousand feet into the sky, the summit was capped by a mantle of snow. Some of its lower slopes were heavily forested with Douglas fir; others, higher up, lacked any vegetation. A few looked as if they were covered with either mud or hardened lava from previous eruptions.

It made Fargo nervous, being so close to a volcano that might blow at any minute. Nuttall had told him that from time to time Mount Saint Helens gave signs of being active, and there was a local Indian legend that once, long ago, it had spewed smoke and lava, killing hundreds in several nearby villages. Which was yet another reason why no tribe lived in its vicinity. Or so everyone claimed.

Fargo guessed that he was about eight miles from the base of the volcano, skirting a much smaller peak, when to the northwest appeared a sizable lake. Of more interest were the dozen tendrils of smoke that spiraled upward from the west shore. Angling into cover, he slowed to a walk.

He had found the village the war party came from. There were bound to be hunters in the area, or other war parties either leaving or coming back. Fargo advanced cautiously. On coming to a meadow, he stopped to scan the area. It was well he did.

From pines on the other side hiked four women, three carrying baskets, the fourth a deerhide bag similar to a parfleche but not decorated with beads as the Indians living on the Plains were fond of doing. The women were short and broad, as the two warriors had been. Their raven hair was cropped below the shoulders. They all wore plain buckskin dresses. A few copper bracelets and shell earrings were the only jewelry they wore. They were chatting and smiling, on their way to gather berries or roots.

Fargo bent forward and patted the stallion's neck to keep it from nickering. The quartet were bending their steps toward a hill to the southwest. He let them go, and once they were out of sight he cut to the right and went around the meadow rather than across it.

The woods thinned. Fargo stuck to the heaviest timber he could find, easing between trunks spaced so close together that he rubbed his legs against them as he rode past. He had gone several hundred yards from the meadow when low voices alerted him to more Indians. This time there were three men, all wearing the same crude armor the first pair had worn. They carried bows and were armed with long knives sporting hilts crafted from deer or elk antlers.

So far Fargo had seen no evidence that this particular tribe had much contact with whites. None of the women or men had on a single article offered by the fur companies in trade for prime furs. Whoever these people were, they either shunned or hated whites, which did not bode well for William Nuttall and his daughters.

The trio passed within seventy feet of Fargo but never spied him or the Ovaro. When they were well gone and he could no longer hear their voices, Fargo proceeded to a cluster of saplings. He was close to the lake now. Its blue surface rippled in small waves caused by the stiff breeze, while raindrops pattered down without letup, forming thousands of tiny circles.

Looping the reins around a tree no thicker than his wrist, Fargo grabbed the Henry, levered a round into the chamber, and glided toward the conical wooden lodges bordering the shoreline. He had never seen dwellings quite like these. The walls had been made from cedar planks, while the roofs were thatch affairs coated with some sort of pitch.

Dozens of men and women worked busily at tasks ranging from curing hides to making arrows. Out on the lake were fishermen in canoes, while on large wooden platforms scores of fish were being laid out to dry. From a tree hung a buck being butchered by two women. Children scampered about, playing. A half-dozen or so frolicked like seals close to shore, squealing and laughing.

Fargo saw no dogs, which worked in his favor. Among the Sioux, Cheyennes, and others, dogs were as thick as fleas. A man sneaking up on one of their villages had to be sure the wind was just right and must never show himself. He was glad this mystery tribe had none.

Crawling to within a stone's throw of the nearest lodge, Fargo rested the rifle in front of him. It was early afternoon, so he had ample time to pinpoint where the Nuttalls were being held. Their mounts and the remaining pair of packhorses were tied beside a lodge much larger than most of the rest. The chief's, he figured.

Fargo counted twenty-seven lodges. By any standard the tribe was small. Maybe, he mused, they had been driven deep into the interior by stronger tribes and had planted their roots in the one region no one else claimed. It would explain a lot—but not how he was going to get the Nuttalls out of there without bloodshed.

If he could avoid violence, he would. Fargo held no grudge and had no hankering for revenge. The tribe was simply protecting its territory, as any other would do. In their eyes, the Nuttalls were invaders who had refused to pay proper tribute. Like the mountain lion that had slain the sorrel, they were doing what came naturally.

Propping his chin on his folded wrists, Fargo awaited the setting of the sun. He had gone so long without decent sleep that he had to resist an urge to doze. A bustle of activity at the main lodge perked his interest, and when William Nuttall was hauled out by a pair of burly warriors, he brought the Henry to his shoulder.

Eight men ringed the artist. They argued bitterly. A scarred character with a headdress twice the size of everyone else's gestured angrily a number of times and made a slashing motion across his neck. It was not hard to guess what he wanted to do.

117

Nuttall was in bad shape. He hung limply, his head sagging, his shoulders slumped. His face was bruised, his hair disheveled. He did not resist when he was shaken violently and slapped.

Fargo feared the rough treatment would be too much for the man's heart. He fixed a bead on the noisy bastard who yearned to slit the painter's throat. As he did, something moved off to his right. Thinking it must be an Indian, he flattened and looked to see if he had been discovered.

Someone else was crawling toward the village. Someone with flame-red hair and a pair of pistols. Davina Nuttall had eyes only for her father and the warriors abusing him. She extended a revolver.

Fargo lifted a hand to wave and get her attention. He had to stop her from firing unless it was absolutely necessary. Suddenly he froze. Creeping up behind her was a smirking warrior.

The man clutched a knife. Another few steps and he would be close enough to use it.

11

Skye Fargo had to do something and do it fast. But no matter what he did, he risked putting the redhead and himself in grave peril. Shooting the warrior would bring the villagers swarming out like riled hornets, and they would be overwhelmed before they reached the Ovaro. If he yelled to warn Davina, the same thing would happen.

Whatever action Fargo took had to be done quietly. But if he rushed to her aid, he stood the risk of being spotted by one of the men near the large lodge or another tribesman, or of having the warrior with the knife spot him and bellow to alert those in the village.

As the old adage went, Fargo was caught between a rock and a hard place. He couldn't just lie there. He couldn't allow Davina to be captured or killed. That was not in his nature.

Pushing into a crouch, Fargo sped toward them. He kept vegetation between himself and the village and angled to the right to come up on the warrior from the rear. Suddenly the man stopped, planted both feet, and raised the knife to strike. Fargo still had twenty feet to cover and there was a low limb in his way. Sinking to one knee, he whipped out the Arkansas toothpick, then reversed his grip so that he held the slim throwing knife by the tip of the blade. He saw the warrior's muscle tighten for the thrust.

"Hey!" Fargo whispered.

The man whirled.

Countless hours of practice had honed Fargo's skill to a high degree. But this was a long throw, twice as far as the ten-foot range he normally paced off. And he had that limb to take into account. Snapping forward, he flashed his right hand in a precise arc.

The warrior was opening his mouth when the keen blade sliced into his throat. He gurgled and staggered, then recovered his balance and lifted his head to yell. At that instant Davina Nuttall sprang. From her boot she had yanked a dagger, which she speared into the warrior, high on his left side close to the edge of his crude armor. The man jerked around, dropping his own weapon, and pawed at the two blades embedded in him. Weakening rapidly, he glanced at the village and started to shuffle toward it.

Fargo was on him before the warrior took two steps. Wrapping his arms around the man's chest, he bore them both to the earth. The warrior struggled. Davina was there in a heartbeat, clamping a hand over the Indian's mouth to keep him from crying out. Glaring at both of them, the warrior made a supreme effort to break free but could not. The spark of life flickered from his eyes as he slowly went limp and expired.

Davina wearily sat up. Her features were haggard from lack of sleep, and her formerly flawless skin was covered with tiny nicks, scratches, and grime. Her clothes were rumpled, her boots covered with mud. "I've never been so glad to see anyone in my life," she whispered.

Fargo wanted to learn how she had gotten there, but just then a harsh shout rent the air. Her father was being lugged to a small lodge closer to the lake, and the scarred warrior did not seem any too happy about it. Nuttall was roughly tossed inside. The two brawny warriors then took up posts on either side of the entrance. The others dispersed, the man with the jagged mark on his face scowling at anyone and everyone.

If Fargo had to hazard a guess, he would say that Scar, as he dubbed the scowler, was a medicine man of some kind. Scar wanted Nuttall slain, but apparently some of the other leading men did not, so the artist had been thrown in the smaller lodge for safekeeping. For the time being, Nuttall would be all right.

Fargo nodded at Davina. "Follow me." Wrenching the toothpick out, he wiped the blade clean on the grass, replaced it, and made off through the brush. She did as he wanted without complaint, and soon they reached the stallion. Fargo swung up, offered his hand, and boosted her up behind him. She leaned against his back as if she were so tired that she would fall off without support.

While spying on the village, Fargo had noticed a finger of land that poked into the lake about two hundred yards beyond it, forming a small peninsula choked with vegetation. It was an ideal spot to lay low until dark. He swung wide to the east, constantly on the lookout for villagers and careful not to venture into the open, where he could be seen by the fishermen out in canoes. Once he had to duck into a thicket to hide from a group of young women on their way back from foraging.

Davina was no chatterbox as her sister was. She rested a cheek on his shoulder, her warm body nestled against his, her breath lightly fanning his neck. When he shifted he could feel her firm breasts. It took some doing to keep his thoughts on the matter at hand.

At last the stallion entered the tall pines on the peninsula. Fargo saw no sign of footpaths. Evidently the Indians rarely came there, which suited him just fine. Well back from the shore, he reined up.

The redhead slid off and walked to a boulder. Sitting, she stared glumly toward the village. "If anything happens to them, I'll never forgive myself."

Ground-hitching the stallion, Fargo cradled the Henry and squatted beside her. "They should be fine until we get them out of there," he said, trying to sound more confident than he felt. "Care to tell me what happened?"

Davina nodded and idly rubbed a bruise on her left wrist. "They hit us about four in the afternoon. Father was sketching and sis was rubbing down that mare she's so fond of. We had finished our coffee so I went to the creek for more water. Suddenly the Indians were everywhere. They were on my father before he could stand. Melissa had left her rifle by the fire, so they had no problem taking her prisoner."

"And you?" Fargo prompted when she stopped.

"I was on my knees, dipping the coffeepot into the creek. Five of them jumped me before I could pull a gun, so I walloped one with the pot and threw water in the face of the next bastard, who had a heavy club. I snatched it from him and started swinging." Davina looked down at her hands. "Don't ask me how, but I kept them at bay. I think they held back a little because they wanted to take me alive. One managed to get his arms around my legs and I fell into the water. They were all over me then, but the gravel bottom was so slippery that none of us could keep our feet. They clipped me a few times, though. I managed to reach the other side and ran into the forest."

"You did well," Fargo complimented her, and meant it. Few people, even seasoned frontiersmen, could fight off five warriors at one time.

"Like hell," Davina said. "I ended up hiding in a hole in a dead tree while the savages searched all over for me. They gave up after half an hour or so and left." The corners of her mouth dipped. "I failed my father and sister, Skye. I shouldn't have let down my guard like I did."

"I don't see what else you could have done," Fargo tried to comfort her.

"Don't patronize me. I should have kept my rifle handy at all times and made sure my sister stood watch while I went for the water." Davina punched her right fist into her left palm. "I was too damn careless and they paid the price."

"They're still alive," Fargo pointed out, "so don't give up hope." Standing, he scanned the lake. The nearest canoe was hundreds of yards off and posed no threat.

"I followed as soon as they were out of sight," Davina went on. "I was afraid if I didn't, I'd lose them." She wiped at a red bang drooping over an eye. "They didn't stop once all night. I guess they wanted to be long gone when you came back." Davina looked up. "Say, I almost forgot. Did you ever find the sorrel?"

"Yes. But a mountain lion found it first." Fargo walked to the Ovaro and helped himself to a handful of pemmican. "When was the last time you had a bite to eat?"

"At breakfast yesterday." Davina accepted some pemmican and began to wolf it down.

"Take your time," Fargo advised. "You can make yourself sick if you eat too fast." He munched slowly while studying the outline of the shore bordering the village. Seven canoes had been pulled onto dry land and lined up in a row. Several men using special tools were at work fashioning a new one from a long log.

"Do you have any idea how we can get them out of there without bringing the whole village down on our heads?" Davina asked.

"I'm working on it," Fargo said. He indicated a clear space under a nearby tree. "Why don't you get some rest while I keep watch? We have five hours to kill before we can do anything."

"I doubt I can sleep," Davina said. "I'm too damn worried." She walked over anyway and curled up on the soft carpet of needles and grass. Her eyes lingered on him. "It's too bad you have wanderlust in your veins. If you were inclined to settle down, I'd give Melissa a run for her money."

Fargo plunked himself down on the boulder she had vacated to ponder what to do. In a short while snoring came from under the tree. He smiled, fetched his bedroll, and covered her with a blanket. Stifling a yawn, he took the Henry and stealthily stalked as close to the lake as he could without giving himself away.

The fishermen were out where the lake fed into a river. Instead of lines, they employed basket-type traps over six feet in length. Each was wide at one end and narrowed to a blunt tip. As near as he could tell, the idea was to lower the traps with the open ends facing into the current. Fish blundering into the baskets were unable to get out.

On the shore a number of boys were playing a game with a hoop and a pole. One would roll the hoop as fast as he could and another would try to hook it before it fell over. They were having a grand time, but their play was slowly bringing them closer to the peninsula.

The village itself was quiet. There was no activity around either the large lodge where he figured Melissa was being held or the smaller one her father had been tossed into. He saw no sign of Scar. An idea came to him, and for a while he studied the shoreline and the woods on the other side of the dwellings. A squeal reminded him of the five boys.

They were much too close for comfort. A skinny sprout of ten or so had the hoop. Bending, he placed it on the ground and pushed. It rolled swiftly past another boy, who tried to spear it with the pole. Wobbling crazily, it came to within six feet of the bush shielding Fargo, then flopped over.

Fargo held himself rigid, not even blinking, as a taller boy dashed over to retrieve the hoop. When the young Indian straightened, he glanced into the trees and hesitated as if he had seen something that had caught his eye. Was it the Ovaro? Fargo wondered. He couldn't twist his head to find out, not with the boy so close that he could extend the Henry and touch one of his legs.

Several of the others shouted. The tall one gave a shrug and tossed the hoop to a friend. All five jogged toward the village, joking and carefree.

Fargo swiveled around. The pinto was nowhere in sight. He scooted into the undergrowth, rose among a bunch of ferns, and moved to a wide pine with many stout low limbs. Leaning the rifle against the bole, he climbed and sat where he could keep track of the comings and goings of those in the village, plus watch the men in the canoes.

Suddenly the tree swayed. Fargo looked down and saw the Henry shake. Bushes and surrounding trees were doing the same. He heard no sound other than the creaking of the trunk. In seconds the swaying stopped, leaving him puzzled. Had it been an earthquake? Or the volcano? He looked toward Mount Saint Helens but could not see the summit due to low clouds.

The Indians acted as if nothing had happened.

Fargo shook his head. The sooner he was out of there, the happier he'd be. In his opinion living near a volcano was a lot like wrestling alligators for a living. Anyone who did it was just asking for an early grave.

Once again, rain fell in a steady drizzle. Fargo had been soaked for so long that he hardly gave it a second thought. Being wet was like breathing—he took both for granted.

About half an hour before sunset, Fargo climbed down. A short while ago all the women and girls had gone into lodges to prepare the evening meal for their families. The men and boys drifted in slowly. He had watched the fishermen paddle across the lake and stow their canoes with the rest. Now the village was quiet and peaceful. Smoke curled from practically every dwelling. The time had come.

Davina Nuttall was still asleep. She had rolled onto her back and was breathing through parted lips so cherry-red that Fargo had an urge to lean down and nibble on them. He nudged her shoulder with a toe. Like a striking sidewinder, she leaped up and stabbed a hand to a pistol. On seeing him, she grinned and relaxed. "Sorry. I thought you were one of the savages."

"I have a plan worked out," Fargo informed her, then detailed it at great length. She listened intently, nodding when he was done.

"It just might work. But if it doesn't, you know where that leaves you. Why don't we change places? It's my father and sister, after all."

"Have you ever used a canoe?"

"No," Davina confessed. "Never had occasion to. In the Everglades we hired a boat."

"It takes a certain knack. You don't just climb in one and paddle." Fargo folded his blanket, then led her to the stallion. "Let him sniff you so he gets used to your scent." She did as he told her while he tied down his bedroll. "Now climb on."

The Ovaro was downright finicky about having anyone but Fargo on top. The Trailsman held the bridle and led the pinto around for a few minutes, all the time stroking its neck and speaking softly to reassure it. When he let go, Davina continued to ride in a small circle so the stallion would get used to her. She stopped when Fargo gestured.

"This is one fine animal, Skye," she said, patting its side. "It has a nice gait."

A distant peak eclipsed the sun. Twilight claimed the Cascades. Lengthening shadows spread across the lake. The lodges resembled dark mounds, the gloom broken by shafts of light from the fires within.

Fargo shoved the Henry into the boot. "I don't want to get it wet," he explained. Stripping off his gun belt, he made a loop of the belt and slung it over his right shoulder so the pistol rested next to his ear. The toothpick he left where it was, since a little water wouldn't harm the tempered steel. He put a hand on Davina's thigh and she kissed him on the forehead.

"What's that for?"

"Being you." The redhead reined the stallion around. "You take care, big man."

Fargo did not move until she was lost among the pines, then he hastened to the lake. It was still much too light for him to make his move, so he went to ground at the same spot as before. Only when night cloaked the land did he stride boldly to the water's edge. The lake was ice-cold. As he slipped into it, he could not help but shiver violently. Stroking quietly, he swam into deeper water.

With the rain pattering down around him, it was difficult for Fargo to hear anything. The far-off howl of a wolf, muffled by the drizzle and distorted by distance and the encircling mountains, sounded a lot like a war whoop. He had to stop and listen closely to identify it for what it was. Going on, he relied on his memory to tell him exactly when to turn toward shore.

The village was virtually invisible in the dark. Fargo had to peer long and hard to distinguish the lodges. It helped him some when a warrior entered the big lodge and left the flap open. The light spilling out revealed the tethered horses and several other dwellings.

Soon Fargo saw a series of bumps lining the lake—the canoes, he realized, and glided cautiously toward them. Without warning, something brushed against his left leg. He stopped, thinking he had bumped into a submerged object, perhaps a log or a boulder. Then the object slammed into him so forcefully that his legs were swatted to the right. It was as if a giant fish had brushed against him.

Fargo doubted that it posed a threat. Like most men who had lived among Indians any length of time, he was familiar with the many tales they told of mysterious monsters that dwelled in certain lakes and rivers. He had never seen one himself, but he knew a mountain man who swore that twenty years earlier he had observed a huge snakelike creature in a lake up north in the Okanogan Valley. The Indians would never cross that lake unless they first tossed a small dead animal in as an offering to the beast.

Shaking his head to dispel his foolish notion, Fargo swam until his boots touched bottom. Here he paused to catch his breath. His waterlogged buckskins and boots had weighed him down so badly that staying afloat had sapped his strength.

Moving slowly so as not to splash, Fargo moved to the first canoe. It had been turned over, so he had to right it without making any sound, then shove it to the water's edge and give it a push hard enough to propel it out toward the middle, but not so hard that he made enough noise to attract attention. One by one he did the same with all the canoes except the last. This one he dragged to the water, but he did not let it slip in.

Just as Fargo finished, voices sounded. Men from every lodge were gathering in the middle of the village. Ten or twelve moved toward the largest structure, among them the man Fargo called Scar. At the entrance they stopped. Scar barked commands and the pair guarding William Nuttall dragged him out and joined the rest. As they entered, Nuttall stumbled when Scar fell into step behind him and gave him a push.

Shrugging the gun belt off his arm, Fargo strapped it around his waist. He checked the Colt by feel alone. No water had dampened the cylinder or the trigger mechanism, so he need not worry about the pistol fouling when he needed it the most.

Hugging the blackest shadows, Fargo cat-footed to the small lodge, in which Nuttall had been held. He pressed an ear to several planks but heard no voices or any hint of movement. Drawing the six-shooter, he dashed to the entrance and slipped into the dark interior. No one was there. So far, all was going according to plan.

Fargo let his eyes adjust before he made a circuit of the single room. Belongings lined the walls, but from the dust on them he gathered that no one had lived there in quite some time. He collected an armful of leather bags and clothes and

127

whatever else he deemed flammable, piling them next to the east wall. From under his hat he took the tinder he had placed there before Davina rode off. From his shirt pocket he took his fire steel and flint. Placing the punk at the edge of the pile, he struck the steel against the small piece of flint. Sparks flew, but none landed in the kindling. Fargo tried again, and a third time. Some of the tinder smoldered. Bending, he puffed lightly, fanning the tiny flames, and fed dry wood shavings he had brought along for that purpose. Gradually the flames grew in size. They ate at the clothes under them and spread up the pile, raising smoke.

Satisfied the fire would not go out, Fargo put the steel back into his pocket and hurried to the entrance. He looked both ways before dashing out and around the lodge. No shouts rang out. No one challenged him as he jogged to the lake and flattened.

It took a while for the flames to ignite the planks. But when they did, the wood went up quickly. Dancing sheets of red and orange shot into the crisp night air, devouring one whole side and licking their way up the roof. Suddenly a woman screeched. Every last occupant of the village poured out to see what the fuss was about. The men converged on the burning lodge, but there was little they could do. It was too far gone.

Bathed in a feeble glow, Fargo stared at the forest, wishing Davina would play her part before one of the Indians turned around and spotted him. All would be lost if that happened. As if she had read his thoughts, hooves drummed in the forest to the east. A horse and rider materialized. The night rocked to the blast of a pistol, the slugs kicking up dirt at the feet of several startled Indians. Shouting and hollering like a she-devil, the redhead wheeled the stallion and plunged back into the woods.

As Fargo had predicted, every last warrior raced in pursuit. The women, believing the village was under attack, scattered to their lodges, driving their children ahead of them. In no time at all, Fargo was alone. He sprinted to the horse string and hastily untied them. Holding the reins of three of them in one hand and two in the other, he pulled the animals toward the vegetation to the north. Gaining cover, he stopped. Precious seconds went by. Just when he thought something had gone wrong, Davina Nuttall burst out of the brush. She had his rope out and ready as he had instructed her to.

Darting from horse to horse, Fargo threw a loop over each animal, then handed the end of the rope to the redhead. "Get going," he said. "I'll meet you on the other side of the lake in an hour."

Davina galloped off. To the east the warriors were yelling back and forth, trying to figure out where she had gotten to.

Fargo spun and ran to the large lodge. For his ruse to work, the warriors had to pick up Davina's trail and follow it on around the end of the lake, buying him the time he needed to cross in the last canoe.

The flap still hung open, so Fargo ducked and slipped inside. He counted on all the warriors being gone. To his left he heard a commotion, and pivoted. Melissa and William Nuttall both lay on thick robes, their hands bound behind their backs. The daughter was on her back, the front of her dress ripped wide-open. Astride her, his hands probing between her legs, was Scar. The warrior leaped up as Fargo turned, then grabbed a war club from the ground and attacked.

12

Skye Fargo automatically went for his Colt. He swept the revolver up and out, but as he did the warrior swung the war club and it smashed into his gun hand. Intense pain shot up his arm. His fingers went numb. Against his will, the Colt dropped. He tried to scoop it up with his other hand but Scar swung again, driving him back.

Melissa and William Nuttall struggled to sit up. Both were gagged, Melissa panting from her effort to fight off the warrior. She heaved to her knees, her mouth working in an attempt to spit out the gag.

All this Fargo took in while retreating before Scar's onslaught. The jagged slash on the man's face had turned a livid red and grew more so the longer Scar exerted himself. Fargo ducked, heard the club swish over his head, then twisted and rammed a fist into the man's temple.

Scar staggered, then shook off the blow and circled. He sneered, perhaps out of confidence he would win since his body armor protected him from serious harm. Or so he thought.

Fargo, in looking around for something he could use as a weapon, laid eyes on a canoe paddle propped against the wall. He skipped toward it while evading the war club. Scar guessed his intent and leaped to cut him off, but Fargo was quicker. Gripping the paddle at either end, he parried a thrust meant to crush his throat. Then he reversed direction, slamming the wide end of the paddle into Scar's face. The warrior nearly went down.

Stumbling, Scar dug in his heels. Blood trickled from the

corner of his mouth. He spat more out at his feet, hefted the club, and growled something in the tongue of his people.

The words were foreign to Fargo but the meaning was pretty clear. He went on the offensive, anxious to finish it before any of the warriors out hunting for Davina returned. Right and left he rained the paddle down, but Scar blocked him every time. Suddenly Scar shouted at the top of his lungs, trying to draw the attention of other villagers. Fargo waded in with the paddle flying to keep the man so busy he wouldn't have time to call out. It worked, but crafty Scar retreated toward the entrance.

Fargo had to stop him from escaping. He lanced the paddle at the warrior's chest, knowing full well it would inflict little pain but hoping it would knock Scar off balance and give him a chance to finish their clash with a blow or two to the head. It worked, in that Scar tottered. But when Fargo arced the paddle back to deliver the telling swing, Scar managed to clip him on the knee.

It was only a glancing hit, yet sheer agony flared up Fargo's leg, and the limb buckled out from under him. Scar seized the moment and loomed over him, flailing like a madman. Fargo raised the paddle, warding off jarring blow after blow until the club struck the fingers of his left hand. Like his leg, it went numb, and Scar's next swing sent the paddle flying.

Fargo looked up into the man's blazing eyes as the warrior elevated the club for a final time. He knew his head would be crushed to a pulp if the club descended. In desperation he shoved upward and caught hold of Scar's nose ring. The warrior jerked his head back but Fargo held on, rotated his wrist, yanked, and heaved. He wanted to flip Scar over his shoulder. Instead, the nose ring sheared through the bottom of the warrior's nostrils, tearing them partway off.

Scar howled and danced aside. He covered his ruined nose with a hand, quaking with torment.

Springing, Fargo seized the war club and tore it from the warrior's grip. Scar flung himself to the left. A flick of Fargo's leg tripped him, and he fell onto his hands and knees. Fargo bunched his shoulder muscles as Scar started to glance up. The club cleaved downward in a blur. There was a sickening crunch, a strangled gasp, and the stocky warrior slumped over with his brains oozing from his shattered skull.

Quickly Fargo cast the club away and picked up the Colt. The toothpick made short shrift of the leather thongs binding Melissa. She embraced him, her eyes watering. Shaking his head, Fargo pushed her back and said, "There's no time for that now. We have to get the hell out of here. Your sister led the rest of the men off, but some might come back at any time." He removed her gag and received a wet kiss on his cheek.

"I understand," she said huskily. "Let's go, then."

William Nuttall was in a bad way. He had been severely beaten. Bruises and welts covered his face and neck. When Fargo freed him, he collapsed and would have fallen had Fargo not braced him up.

"Can you walk?"

"I can try," the artist gamely replied.

Fargo had Melissa bring the paddle while he supported her father. The small lodge was engulfed in flames that spurted high into the sky, casting a glow bright enough to light up half the village. As yet none of the women or children had reappeared. To save time, he made a beeline for the shore. As they passed another dwelling, a child's head popped out. The boy recoiled in stark terror and vanished inside. His shrill cries inspired Fargo to go faster. Practically carrying Nuttall, he reached the canoe and eased the man down in the middle. "Stay low," he directed.

Melissa helped push the canoe into the lake. Fargo had her kneel in front of her father, then he guided the canoe farther out so his added weight wouldn't cause it to scrape bottom. When the water was up to his waist he swung into the stern. Melissa passed him the paddle and he began pumping his arms in powerful, even strokes.

A knot of women had formed in the village. Several held bows. There was a lot of excited jabbering and pointing. Then, in a body, they ran to the water where they railed and shook their fists in impotent fury.

Fargo paddled harder. Two of the women had stepped forward and were notching arrows to sinew strings. Ordinarily, in most tribes, women did not engage in warfare unless their village was raided. There were many instances in which they had fought fiercely in defense of their people. What they lacked in skill they more than made up for in their savage devotion to their loved ones.

Glancing over a shoulder, Fargo saw the women raise their bows to take aim. The canoe was dreadfully close to the shore, well within range. Fortunately, the glow from the burning lodge did not quite reach that far. They would not be easy targets. As he bent to dip the paddle, he heard twin twangs. An arrow splashed into the water a few yards to his left. The other one whizzed well above his head and sliced into the frigid water farther out.

The women broke out in howls of glee. Fargo assumed it was because they mistakenly believed they had hit him. Then he spotted several warriors racing through the village. There was a brief exchange, and all three swiftly stripped off their armor and their helmets, then dived in.

The men propelled themselves through the water like sleek otters. They were remarkably fast, stroking their arms so smoothly that they hardly made any ripples.

The canoe knifed westward. Fargo paddled first on the right side, then on the left. He was tired from having gone so long without sleep, but he did not let that slow him down. If he faltered, the warriors would catch up and dump them all in the lake.

The rain had almost stopped, but a stiff wind from the northwest buffeted the canoe, pushing against the bow like a giant invisible hand, slowing them down. Fargo, stooped over, was doing his best, yet it wasn't good enough.

"They're gaining!" Melissa said.

She was right. Already the trio had covered half the distance. One man, in particular, cut through the water as if he were more fish than human. Clenched between his teeth was a long knife.

Between the wind and his own fatigue, Fargo did not stand

a prayer. He reached deep within himself, tapping the reservoir of stamina that had never let him down yet. His shoulders protested, but he paddled with redoubled vigor, his paddle swishing in a steady cadence. It was not good enough.

"Look out, Skye!" the black-haired beauty cried.

The fleetest swimmer was almost on top of them. Fargo turned as the man took the knife from his mouth and lunged. Bronzed fingers closed on the rim. The man went to pull himself in. Instantly Fargo snapped the paddle around, catching the warrior across the chest and knocking him into the water. In the time it took the warrior to resurface, Fargo gained another ten feet.

A second warrior flew past the first. This one did not have a knife, but the set of his jaw showed that he did have determination. He grasped hold and gave the canoe a shake. Fargo brought the paddle crashing down on his fingers. Yowling, he released them and began to tread water.

Only one warrior still gave chase and he was the slowest of the three. Fargo smiled as he began to pull ahead, but his smile was short-lived, for the very next moment the canoe rocked as if it had struck a submerged obstacle. It nearly tipped over. Melissa cried out and grabbed her father, who had slumped forward, barely conscious.

Fargo didn't know what to make of it. He was in open water. The fishermen had safely passed through that very part of the lake shortly before the sun sank. So what could he have hit? Another loud thump on the bottom made the canoe pitch as if it were a bucking bronco. Whatever it was, it was repaying the favor. He remembered the thing that had bumped against him when he swam from the peninsula and figured it had to be the same animal.

Melissa jabbed a finger. "There's another one!"

The last warrior had overtaken them. He had a tomahawk, which he raised on high. Suddenly the man bobbed down into the water as if he were a cork. Or as if something lurking in the depths had tried to pull him under. He uttered a frightened squawk.

Fargo was going to go on when the water around the warrior

churned and roiled. A scaly hump broke the surface, either the back of a fish or part of some other creature. The warrior screamed and faced his companions. They were paralyzed with fear and made no move to help him. When a second hump appeared closer to them, they streaked toward shore, shouting the same name over and over again. To Fargo, it sounded as if they were saying, "Khir-lit!"—whatever that meant.

"Get us out of here!" Melissa urged.

The third Indian started to follow his fellows. He had taken three strokes when he stiffened and flung his arms skyward. A piercing scream tore from his lungs as the creature started to pull him under. The humps slowly sank along with him. He thrashed wildly but his legs were clamped fast and he could not break loose. Twisting and tugging, he slashed the tomahawk into the water again and again, striving to slay whatever had him in its iron grip. The water rose to his neck, to his jaw. He became hysterical.

"God!" Melissa wailed. "What is that thing?"

Fargo didn't know and he wasn't about to linger to find out. He resumed paddling. The warrior was nearly gone, just his nose and eyes and forehead showing. His scream had changed to a ghastly screech, which was abruptly smothered when he was yanked completely under. The lake bubbled and foamed in an ever-widening circle. For a few seconds Fargo thought the canoe would be caught in the upheaval and swamped.

"It's going to get us!" Melissa declared. She held her father tight. "Hang on!"

As abruptly as the roiling began, it ceased. The surface calmed, becoming as smooth as glass. There was no trace of the creature or its victim.

Fargo pushed himself to his limit. They still had a long way to go to reach the other side, and that thing might still be hungry after it was done with the warrior. Time went by. The lake stayed tranquil. He only slowed when the shore was so close that he could see the trunks of individual trees. Raising the paddle, he let the canoe glide the final twenty feet. As the front end grated onto gravel, he leaped out, gripped the side, and pushed until they were out of the water. "We're safe now," he said, breathing heavily from his exertion.

"Are we?" Melissa did not sound so sure. "What if that thing can crawl up on land?"

Fargo straightened. It was a possibility he hadn't considered. And even though common sense told him the creature had to be a huge fish he had never seen before, he was not taking anything for granted. "Get out," he commanded, and gave her a hand walking her father to a log. The canoe he pulled into brush and covered with grass and high weeds. The camouflage would not fool anyone in broad daylight, but it should serve to confuse the Indians in the dark of the night.

"What now?" Melissa asked.

"We wait for your sister to show," Fargo said. It would take Davina a lot longer, since she was going clear on around the north end of the lake. "Another hour and she should be here."

William Nuttall tried to sit up on his own but he was too weak. Melissa propped him against the log and caressed his cheek. "Those rotten devils!" she snapped. "Look at what they've done to you!"

The painter mumbled and sank back. Fargo wondered if he were busted up inside and put the question to the daughter.

"I have no idea. That bastard with the scar kicked him around for a while and there was nothing I could do but lie there and watch." She glanced across the lake where flames still ate at the destroyed lodge. "If you hadn't split his skull, I would have done it myself."

Out on the lake there was a loud splash. Moments later small waves rolled up onto the shore, growing louder as they grew in size.

"It's that thing," Melissa whispered. "It's searching for us."

The idea was preposterous. Still, Fargo looped an arm around William Nuttall and bore him into the forest a short distance to a clearing. He made Nuttall comfortable, then rustled up all the kindling and dry branches he could find. Close to a tree that blocked the wind he built a small fire.

The warmth revived the artist. He opened his eyes and rose on an elbow. "Will wonders never cease. I'm still alive."

"How do you feel, Father?" Melissa asked.

"Sore all over. And I have a nagging pain on my right side. Otherwise, I'm fine." Nuttall placed a hand on her arm. "You were quite brave back there, my dear, the way you stood up to that mean one and fought when he tried to rape you."

"Being feisty runs in the family, or hadn't you noticed?" the daughter joked.

They embraced, and Fargo left them to go to the lake. The surface was serene again. Faintly across the water came a chorus of upraised voices. It sounded as if the Indians were chanting. He surveyed the shoreline to the north without seeing hide nor hair of the redhead or the horses. Had she run into trouble? Had the stallion acted up? He hiked along the beach a few hundred feet and put his ear to the ground but did not hear the rumble of approaching hoofbeats.

William and Melissa were huddled shoulder to shoulder when Fargo rejoined them. Hunkering down, he shook his head when she gave him a questioning look.

The artist was downcast. He held his hands out to warm them and said, "I see now that I was wrong, Mr. Fargo. I should have heeded your advice back in San Francisco. This venture was harebrained. I nearly got all of us killed."

"It's not over yet," Fargo reminded him.

Nuttall seemed to have aged five years in the past twenty-four hours. "It is as far as I'm concerned. My painting supplies are all gone. My brushes were broken, my easel destroyed, my paints scattered. I have no means of painting a blue tanager even if we were to find one. As soon as you want, we might as well head for the Columbia." He frowned. "My last expedition has turned out to be my only failure. Too bad. I would have liked to end my career on a distinguished note."

Melissa squeezed his arm. "Don't despair. Since when does a Nuttall give up? We can try again next year."

"I wish," her father said. "You know as well as I do that my doctor will never permit it. I'll spend the last days of my life moping over what might have been."

Fargo felt sorry for the man but there was nothing he could do. They had lost all their provisions except what little he carried in his saddlebags. Getting them to Portland would be a challenge in itself. "Why don't you turn in," he suggested. "I'll wake you when I hear Davina coming."

Both balked, but Fargo insisted so they stretched out. Soon they were sleeping peacefully. He found it hard to keep his own eyes open and rose to pace several times. Midnight came and went. The redhead should have been there hours ago, which led him to fear the worst. When he could fend off sleep no longer, he sat braced against a tree with his Colt in hand and closed his eyes.

It was shortly after sunrise when Fargo next opened them. He was annoyed at himself for having slept longer than he had wanted. Leaving the Nuttalls to enjoy a little more rest, he hastened to the lake. No Indians were evident, but far out bobbed several of the empty canoes, drifting with the current. To the north nothing moved except several deer slaking their thirst.

William Nuttall was sitting up when Fargo came to the clearing. The artist ran a hand through his rumpled hair, started to yawn, then caught himself and asked, "Davina?"

"No sign of her," Fargo revealed. "Wake up Melissa. We'll work our way back around the lake and look for her trail."

"What if we can't find it?" Nuttall asked in dismay.

"Six horses leave a lot of tracks. She'll have left a trail anyone could follow," Fargo assured him.

Their talk awakened Melissa, who was more upset by her sister's absence than her father had been. They struck off for the north shore right away with Fargo in the lead. Sleep had restored the artist's vim, and he kept up with no problem.

Fargo was always watching for Indians. Some of the canoes were bound to have beached themselves near the village, so he expected to spot warriors patroling the shoreline before the day was very old.

Presently they neared a low ridge that ran down to the water's edge. Fargo motioned for the others to stay put while he climbed the slope to check for nasty surprises on the other side. There was a surprise, all right, but it wasn't nasty. He was dumbfounded to discover the Ovaro and three of the five other horses grazing in a meadow. Beckoning to the Nuttalls, he jogged down to the pinto, which saw him coming and met him halfway.

Fargo grasped the dangling reins and stroked the stallion's neck while moving to the saddle. His rifle was still in the boot and all his gear was intact. The only thing missing was Davina Nuttall. He lifted a foot to a stirrup, then paused. Splattered on the saddle horn and the front third of the saddle were dark blotches. They were drops of blood. And they had not been there the day before.

Melissa and her father were almost out of breath when they got there. They separated to gather their horses, Melissa going to the mare she favored so much. Her face as pale as a sheet, she climbed on, saying, "I don't like this one bit. Davina wouldn't let these animals stray off. Something terrible must have happened."

"Hush. Don't talk like that," William said. "Your sister can take care of herself. I'm sure there's a perfectly logical explanation."

Fargo was not so sure. He kept the blood a secret for the time being. The pair were upset enough without adding to their misery. Taking charge of the spare horse, he trotted toward the extremely thick woodland adjoining the north end of the lake. The clouds had yet to break. Somber and gray, they promised more rain before the day was gone. Rearing grim and menacing over them was Mount Saint Helens.

Backtracking into the trees, Fargo looked for a sign of what had happened to the other two horses. A quarter of a mile in, he found where they had parted company with the rest. As best as he could make out from the prints, all the horses had been fleeing in a panic when the pair had veered to the northwest.

Fleeing from what, though? That was the question. Fargo soon came to the base of a hill choked with manzanita. A single gnarled tree grew at the top. Since the trail wound up and over, so did he. Halfway to the crest he spied a boot poking out of a clump of weeds below a low limb. Spurring the pinto to the spot, he vaulted off.

Davina Nuttall lay on her right side, her face covered by her red mane. Her coat had been torn. Blood caked the collar.

Fargo gently turned her over and carefully moved the hair aside. A four-inch gash on the left side of her forehead explained the blood. Relief coursed through him when her chest expanded.

Melissa dropped down beside him. "Sis!" she wailed, lifting Davina's head into her lap.

William Nuttall was only a few steps behind. He felt Davina's pulse and checked for fever, then lightly shook her shoulder. The redhead groaned. He shook both shoulders, and this time her eyes fluttered open.

"Where—? What—?" Davina croaked.

Before anyone could answer, Fargo felt the earth under him move as it had the day before when he was in the pine. Several of the horses whinnied. The tree next to them swayed. He figured an earthquake was the culprit. Then, behind him, rose a tremendous rumbling roar, like the peal of a dozen thunderclaps booming all at once.

Fargo whirled.

Smoke was billowing from Mount Saint Helens.

13

Melissa Nuttall took the words right out of Fargo's mouth when she exclaimed, "The volcano is erupting! We're done for!"

The ground shuddered again, much worse than before, as if it were about to burst open and swallow them. Thicker smoke spewed from the mountain. High up, a number of huge boulders were dislodged and tumbled to lower slopes. Every living thing within earshot had fallen silent, except the horses.

Fargo gathered the reins of each animal in hand before any of them took it into their heads to run off.

"Now be calm, everyone," William Nuttall said. "Major eruptions are very rare. I doubt very much that Mount Saint Helens is about to blow. More than likely it will puff and rumble a while and then calm down."

"If you say so," Melissa said, but she did not sound as if she believed him.

For Fargo's part, he wanted to get the hell out of there. They had enough to worry about, what with the Indians and the loss of all their provisions. The volcano going active was the last straw. "Mount up," he ordered. "I want to be as far from this place as we can by nightfall."

"But what about Davina?" William protested. "She's in no condition to travel."

The redhead had sat up and was holding a hand to her forehead. "No, Father," she said through clenched teeth. "It's all right. Skye has a point. We're too close to the village. After what we did, those savages will not give up searching for us for days." She attempted to rise but her knees buckled. Melissa

141

caught her and held her until she steadied herself. "Sorry. I'm a little dizzy."

"I insist we wait," the artist declared. "At least a little while, so Davina can recover. What harm can half an hour do?"

The question was addressed to Fargo. He stared at Mount Saint Helens, which had stopped rumbling, and off through the forest to the east. No Indians were abroad, and since they were a good two miles from the village, he reckoned they would be safe enough. "But only thirty minutes," he said. "No more than that."

Melissa helped her sister slide back to lean against the tree. Davina probed the gash, flinching.

"What happened, precious?" William asked, taking the redhead's other hand. "Did one of those awful Indians do this to you?"

"My own stupidity did," Davina answered. "I was making good time, like Skye wanted me to, when I noticed that several of the horses were lagging. The lead rope needed to be shortened, so I stopped." She licked her lips and winched. "I took the rope off. All the horses were standing there behaving themselves when a bear rushed out of a nearby thicket. I couldn't tell if it was a grizzly or a black. The damn thing reared up and growled, and all the horses took off. I jumped on the Ovaro."

William pointed to her wound. "Did the bear do this?"

"No," Davina said. "It never laid a claw on me." She indicated the low limb above them. "I was so intent on catching the horses that I didn't see the branch until I was right on top of it. I tried to duck but it was too late."

"Thank God you're alive," William said, hugging her. "That's all that matters, as far as I'm concerned."

"Me, too, sis," Melissa added.

Fargo was scouring the woodland. Through a gap in the pines he could see the lake about a quarter of a mile away. Suddenly a canoe containing five or six warriors sailed into view, bearing to the west. They were close to shore, scanning the undergrowth.

William Nuttall stood. "Say, what about the two horses still missing? Shouldn't one of us go after them?"

Fargo knew who he meant. "They're on their own," he said. "We're sticking together until we're safe and sound in Portland." The tone he used must have told them that he would brook no argument, because none of them saw fit to dispute the issue. He tied the reins, then took the Henry and prowled the immediate vicinity. A faint shout to the south drew his gaze to a second crammed canoe traveling in the same direction as the first. The Indians were out in force, thirsting for their blood.

Melissa had torn a strip from the bottom of her sister's shirt and was tying a makeshift bandage over the gash when Fargo approached. "We can't wait half an hour," he informed them, and looked at the redhead. "Think you can manage if we leave now?"

"I'm no weakling," Davina stated. She rose without help but had to prop herself against the trunk for a few moments before she could shuffle to her mount. Her father and sister aided her in getting on and stood beside the horse until she nodded that she was ready.

"I don't like this one bit," the artist muttered at Fargo as he walked to his own animal. "She's apt to fall off before we've gone a hundred yards."

"I'll be fine," Davina spoke up. "It won't take long for my head to clear. So quit pestering Skye. He's right and we all know it."

Fargo headed out to forestall more petty bickering. Melissa stayed close to the redhead, while their father brought up the rear. They rode well shy of the lake. Whenever Fargo came to an opening in the trees he looked for more canoes, but he did not see any. He mentally crossed his fingers that the Indians would follow the shoreline on around to their village.

Smoke continued to billow above the volcano, but there were no more tremors. Birds chirped and flitted about again, while squirrels and chipmunks scampered everywhere.

When Fargo judged that they had passed the northwest corner of the lake, he angled to the south and looked back to see how the others were faring. Davina and Melissa were talking softly, the redhead riding tall in the saddle. William Nuttall, to his amazement, was gone. Fargo hauled on the reins, swinging the stallion around. "Where's your father?" he demanded.

The women were as startled as Fargo.

"He was right behind us a minute ago," Melissa said. "I saw him."

Davina, rising in her stirrups, jabbed a finger. "There he is!" she declared. "What does he think he's doing?"

Fargo wondered the same thing. Nuttall was riding swiftly toward the lake, bobbing and bending his head as if he were trying to see something in the distance. "Stay here," Skye growled, breaking into a trot. He didn't call out for fear the Indians in the canoes might hear if they were near. Unexpectedly, the artist reined up, jumped down, and dashed off into the pines on foot. "What the hell?" Fargo said to himself. He covered the final thirty feet to Nuttall's mount, sprang to the ground, and sped after the idiot.

The man was doing the same thing he had done on the horse, namely bobbing up and down and leaning to the right and left. He seemed almost frantic in his efforts to see whatever had caught his interest, without any regard for how much noise he was making.

Soon the shore appeared. Fargo ran flat out to overtake the artist before Nuttall blundered into the open. Suddenly Nuttall stopped and turned to the left, his arms outstretched, his face aglow with inner rapture. Fargo slowed and looked in the same direction the painter was looking. For a few moments he saw nothing out of the ordinary. Then a small bird appeared, hopping from one limb to another. It was the size and shape of a tanager. And it was a brilliant hue of blue.

William Nuttall's prayers had been answered.

Fargo stopped and grinned. He had never seen anyone get so excited over a bird before. Nuttall stared, transfixed, as if he had found the Holy Grail. The rare blue tanager warbled a few times, and Fargo half expected Nuttall to break out in tears. Then something moved close to the lake, and Fargo swiveled to see that two canoes had been drawn up on the shore and ten painted Indians in full battle armor had fanned out and were stalking toward Nuttall. As yet they had not spied Fargo.

One of the warriors raised a bow. "Get down!" Fargo bawled, launching himself at the artist.

Simultaneously, three things happened. His yell frightened the tanager into taking wing. Nuttall shifted to follow its flight. And at that selfsame instant, the warrior released the shaft. It missed Nuttall by no more than an inch, thudding into a pine beyond him. Nuttall was so engrossed in the bird that he failed to notice.

Fargo took a few more strides, then dived, tackling the artist with one arm just as several other warriors fired. Shafts zipped above them. One thudded into a trunk to their right.

Nuttall, shocked out of his daze, glanced around and said, "My word! The savages! Where did they come from?"

The Indians were advancing rapidly. Every last one held a bow. Fargo rolled to the nearby tree, raised onto his knees, and fixed a bead on the foremost warrior. Thumbing back the hammer, he held his breath, steadied his arms, and squeezed the trigger. The warrior reacted as if he had been hammered by a battering ram, catapulating backward and lying deathly still. The rest scattered, a few loosing arrows that streaked wide of the mark.

"We've got to get out of here!" Nuttall cried, and went to stand.

"Stay down, damn it!" Fargo bellowed. "You won't get ten feet." He sighted on a second warrior skulking through a thicket toward them. Working the Henry's lever, he sighted on the man's chest. At the booming retort of the rifle, the warrior folded in half.

The remaining warriors had gone to ground. Fargo snapped off two more shots at random to discourage them, then grabbed Nuttall's arm and retreated deeper into the forest, using all available cover. He wanted to slip away quietly if they could, but Nuttall kept tripping and stumbling, making enough racket for the Indians to pinpoint where they were. They rounded a fir. Before them lay a large log. Fargo gestured for Nuttall to get behind it. He'd lifted a leg to slide over when out of the brush flashed a shaft that embedded itself inches from his knee.

Fargo snapped off a shot at a flitting shadow, then dropped into a crouch next to Nuttall. Even though he had used only five of the fifteen cartridges the Henry held, he quickly replaced the spent rounds.

William Nuttall, true to form, sat with his back to the log, a lopsided grin on his face. "Did you see it, Skye?" he asked dreamily. "Wasn't the tanager magnificent?"

"This is hardly the time or place to be talking about that stupid bird."

"Stupid?" Nuttall said, appalled. "Don't you realize what a rare treat that was? Only a handful of people have ever seen it. I'll treasure the memory always." He rubbed his hands with glee. "Now I can't wait to reach Portland so I can paint it while the image is fresh in my mind."

"You're forgetting something, aren't you?" Fargo asked, and nodded at the encircling trees. "These Indians aren't about to let us go anywhere." He saw no reason to mention that if he were alone, eluding the warriors would be simple.

"What can I do to help?"

"Can you shoot?" Fargo asked, about to draw his Colt and hand it over.

"Not very well, I'm afraid. Those who know me best claim I couldn't hit the broadside of a barn with a cannon."

Changing his mind, Fargo palmed the Arkansas toothpick. "Hold onto this in case they get past me," he said. A swarthy shape materialized off to the left, and Fargo lifted the Henry, but the warrior vanished.

"I don't know," Nuttall said, eyeing the knife as if it were about to bite him. "I've never stabbed anyone before. I honestly don't think I could do it."

Fargo glanced at him. "Don't get squeamish on me. Either we fight or we die. It's that simple." He rested the rifle barrel on top of the log. "I happen to be fond of breathing, myself."

There was no more time for idle talk. Warriors glided through the trees to the north and south in a flanking maneuver. Fargo glimpsed them now and again but could not bring the Henry to bear. "It won't be long," he said softly. "Go for their throats or their bellies."

The forest was still. The Indians were in position. Fargo loosened the Colt in its holster and wiped a sleeve across his brow. He sensed that one or two had snuck behind him but he couldn't see them. They would be the ones to watch for when the attack came.

A strident war whoop was the signal. On all sides warriors appeared, unleashing arrows. Fargo had to duck or be hit, which was exactly what they wanted him to do. It enabled them to rush in close. When he popped up, two of them were almost to the log. His first shot ripped into the fastest man's stomach, spinning the Indian around. His second shot slammed into the shoulder of the other one, who jerked around but did not fall. The man let go of his bow to grab his knife. Snarling like a rabid wolf, he jumped onto the top of the log and went to hurl himself at Fargo. At the blast of the Henry he was lifted from his perch and flung to the ground.

Meanwhile, others converged from different directions. Fargo spun as an arrow clipped the whangs on his shirt. A burly warrior was charging out of the trees to his rear. The Indian had a knife in one hand, a war club in the other. Fargo relied on his Colt, drawing and firing as the man swooped toward him. A hole blossomed in the center of the warrior's chest and he did a pirouette to the grass.

That made five out of five. Shrieking and hollering, the rest were mere strides away from swarming over Fargo and the artist. He turned to fan the Colt as to the west pistols cracked in a steady cadence, four shots in a row. A pair of warriors crashed down.

Davina Nuttall had arrived. A smoking pistol in either hand, she threw herself into the fray, moving stiffly due to her wound. She dropped a third warrior who had whirled to confront her, nailing him with a shot from each pistol at the same time.

Which left two warriors on their feet, one rushing Fargo, another almost on top of William Nuttall. The artist sat glued in place, making no attempt to use the Arkansas toothpick. He might as well have been holding a peashooter for all the good it did him.

Fargo wanted to help the painter, but he had his hands full. He leveled his Colt at the warrior bounding like a panther toward him. The Indian, armed with a stone tomahawk, roared and swung his arm back. Fargo had him dead to rights, but when he squeezed the trigger, all he heard was a metallic click. The tomahawk whisked toward his head. He shifted and ducked, causing the blow to miss. The warrior retreated a step, but instead of swinging again he lowered his shoulders and barreled into Fargo like a bull buffalo.

Unable to brace himself, Fargo grunted as the man's hard helmet gouged into his stomach. He was lifted off his feet and crashed onto the log. For a few moments he teetered, his hands stabbing for purchase. Then the warrior shoved and he fell, hitting on his right elbow on the other side. A shot thundered. And another. He quickly jumped up and pointed the Colt at the warrior, but hesitated. The Indian just stood there, his features blank. Exactly why became clear when the man slumped against the log, revealing the hilt of the toothpick sticking out of his side. The warrior looked at Fargo in mute appeal, his mouth moving soundlessly, his face screwed up in pain. Slowly cocking the pistol, Fargo shot him between the eyes.

The last warrior lay prone a few feet from William Nuttall, a bullet hole in his temple.

The artist had risen to stab the man armed with a tomahawk, and now he stood sagging against the log, blinking at the stabbed Indian as if he could not believe he had done it.

Davina was going from warrior to warrior, insuring they were dead. One shifted and groaned. She walked up to him, touched a pistol to his ear, and fired.

"We did it!" Nuttall blurted in amazement. "We're safe!"

"Not by a long shot," Fargo said. "Others are bound to have heard all the shots. We won't be safe until we're halfway to the Columbia."

Nuttall straightened. "Then what are we waiting for? I've seen the tanager so there's no reason to dally."

Fargo reloaded both the Henry and the Colt, claimed his

throwing knife, then climbed onto the log. Much of the lake was visible, and he spotted a canoe bearing six warriors moving rapidly toward the pair of canoes already beached on shore. In another minute or two they would land. "Make for the horses!" he directed. "Pronto!"

Davina reloaded on the fly. She slowed every so often and once cupped a hand to her head. Fargo went to put an arm around her waist to help her along but she swatted it away, saying, "I can manage by my lonesome, handsome. I don't need a nursemaid. Never have, never will."

Melissa was holding the horses. Everyone mounted, and Fargo took the point, galloping on through the forest until he came to the meadow. From there he saw the third canoe grounded on shore but no sign of the six warriors. In a few moments howls of outrage wafted from the forest.

Reining due south, Fargo stuck to the open belt of land bordering the lake to make better time. To the north, thick smoke continued to billow from towering Mount Saint Helens, while across the lake rose plumes of smoke from a number of lodges in the village. The Indians did not seem the least bit alarmed by the volcano's antics. It was as if they took it for granted and considered it no threat. They would learn better if there was ever an actual eruption.

Despite their ordeal, William Nuttall was in fine spirits once again. He whistled as he rode. And when he wasn't whistling, he was pointing out birds and telling of their habits, just as he had done early on in their journey.

The lake was long and narrow. It took them until shortly before noon to reach the south end. Fargo figured he could relax a little and called a halt to water the animals. He walked over to the redhead, who had removed her bandage and dipped it in the lake water. "I never thanked you for bailing us out back there," he said.

"I couldn't let anything happen to our father," Davina responded. Her eyes twinkling, she added, "Or to a man who can kiss like you. It would be a waste of prime manhood."

Fargo bent to let her know that his lips were at her service any time of the day or night. Suddenly Melissa squealed and jabbed a finger to the northeast.

"More canoes!"

A pair filled with briskly paddling warriors flowed smoothly toward them. They were out of bow range but would not be so for long.

"Mount and ride," Fargo commanded. He allowed the others to go ahead of him.

The Indians became quite vocal when they saw their enemies escaping. They stroked faster. A few loosed arrows that fell short.

Fargo's attention was on the canoes, since that was where he believed the threat to be. A warning yell from Davina proved him wrong. Facing around, he saw a line of armored warriors advancing toward them. Beyond, at the point where the lake flowed into the river, three canoes resting on a strip of grass revealed how the warriors had gotten there. Fargo's mouth compressed into a slit. He should have seen this coming, he told himself. The Indians were bound to have sent men to various points to prevent them from leaving the valley.

The Nuttalls had halted. Fargo rode past William and Melissa to Davina's side. She had pulled both pistols. He drew the Colt, then glanced at the canoe out on the lake. It was almost within bow range now. They were boxed in, with deep water to their left and a steep slope to their right. "We're trapped," he announced. "Our best bet is to fight our way through."

The redhead chuckled. "I wouldn't have it any other way." To her father and sister, she said, "Hug your saddles and ride like hell. Don't stop, no matter what. I'll protect you. I promise."

Fargo glanced at her. Davina nodded. He lashed the Ovaro, breaking into a gallop from a dead start. Her pistol banged before his, and one of the warriors fell. Arrows whistled, raining down around them like hail. He snapped a shot at a man in their path, another at a warrior taking aim at Davina. He dared not look back to see how Nuttall and Melissa were doing. If they fell behind they would pay with their lives.

The warriors in the center of the line stood firm, notching shafts with flying fingers. But as skilled as they were, they could not make arrows fly faster than Fargo and the redhead could shoot. A wall of lead crumpled four of them in the span of seconds.

Fargo was almost to the gap. He only had two cartridges left in the cylinder so he had to make each shot count. A warrior to his left took one in the chest. Then he was past the band and twisted in the saddle to cover Melissa and William. They were eating his dust, William bent so low that the saddle horn poked his neck. Melissa grinned with excitement.

A warrior leaped to intercept them, his war club elevated to strike.

Fargo's last bullet brought the man down. Arrows pelted the ground around them as they rounded a bend. William's mount nickered shrilly, a crimson groove marring its flank. Davina had slowed to fire at three warriors who had not yet given up. Two toppled and the third decided he'd had enough.

Fargo did not judge it safe to stop until they had gone several hundred yards. The artist and Melissa were all smiles at their narrow escape. Davina, oddly, was white as a sheet when she caught up. Fargo couldn't help asking, "Are you all right?"

"No," the redhead said softly. Suddenly she slumped forward, revealing the long feathered shaft stuck in her back.

14

"No!" Melissa Nuttall wailed, and moved her horse alongside her sister's. She grabbed Davina's arm just as Davina began to fall. "Help me!" she cried.

Fargo was off the stallion before William lifted a leg to dismount. He caught Davina and gently lowered her to the ground. She mumbled a few words but did not open her eyes. Drawing the toothpick, he quickly slit her heavy coat on either side of the arrow and gingerly pried the fabric back. Underneath she had on a thick wool shirt and her underthings. Thanks to the layer of clothing, the arrow had not penetrated as deeply as it would have otherwise. The point was embedded a few inches below her right shoulder blade. It had penetrated at an angle, sparing her vital organs.

"We have to get that out!" William urged.

Fargo wanted to, but from around the bend rose the clamor of angry voices. He figured that the other canoe had arrived, and at any moment warriors would appear. "Hear that?" he said, and when the artist and Melissa cocked their heads, he added, "We've got to keep going. The arrow will have to wait until we're in the clear."

William was none too happy. "I suppose you're right," he conceded. "But let's hurry, shall we?"

Fargo already had Davina in his arms. He handed her to her father, swung onto the Ovaro, then bent to hike Davina up in front of him. Thanks to William's help he managed it without jostling her. Melissa caught hold of the reins of Davina's horse, then off they flew. Fargo glanced back when they had gone a few hundred yards and saw a knot of warriors rush around the bend. Howls of frustration were hurled at them.

At a trot they rode to the mouth of the valley and up the ridge from which Fargo had first seen the lake. He turned for one last look. Black clouds of smoke spewed from Mount Saint Helens, spreading out over the water and the village. "If those Indians don't get out of there, they're done for," he remarked.

"Good riddance," Melissa snapped. "After what they've done, I hope every single one of them is roasted alive in red-hot lava."

"Does that include the women and children?"

Melissa's temper flared. "Hell, no. Of course not. Don't go putting words in my mouth. I'm not the barbarian here. You know what I meant."

Fargo rode on, holding Davina close to cushion her. Presently she stirred, looked up, and pursed those lovely lips of hers.

"Damn you. You're doing it again."

"Doing what?" Fargo asked, perplexed.

"Being my big, strong protector. How many times do I have to tell you that I don't need a nursemaid? I'm perfectly capable of riding by myself. So put me down."

Fargo ignored her. Within moments she had passed out again. He stared down at her beautiful face and grinned, then made for a gap between a pair of mountains. Only when they were safely through the pass and had seen no sign of armored warriors did he judge it safe to halt in a clearing beside a swift-flowing stream. He got a fire going while William watered the horses. Pulling the toothpick from its sheath, Fargo held the blade in the flames for over a minute. Then he stood.

Melissa had spread a blanket and placed her sister facedown on it. Kneeling at Davina's side, she nervously regarded the knife as Fargo came over. "Are you sure you can do this? What if your hand slips and you cut a vein?"

"Would you rather do it?" Fargo responded, holding the toothpick out. When she made no answer, he knelt and bent over the redhead.

153

William hustled up. "Please be careful," he said. "If anything should happen to her, I'll never forgive myself."

Fargo was reaching the end of his patience with both of them. "You should have thought of that before you dragged her out here," he said gruffly. "Now let's get to it."

They removed Davina's coat, pulling it up off the arrow once they had slid her arms out of the sleeves. Fargo cut the shirt and her underthings, exposing her skin. By probing with his fingers, he could tell that the tip of the arrow was embedded about two inches. He gripped the shaft, placed his other hand flat against her shoulder blade, and tried to pull the arrow out. It wouldn't budge.

"What's wrong?" William Nuttall asked. "Why won't it come loose?"

"I'll show you in a bit," Fargo said. "Hold her in case she comes to. This is going to hurt." They looked at one another, then each took one of the redhead's arms. Inserting the very tip of the blade into Davina's flesh next to the shaft, Fargo slowly cut downward to where the barbed bone point was snagged on a layer of muscle. "See?" he said. "We're just lucky it didn't wedge in a bone. A man by the name of Jim Bridger once went about three years with an arrowhead in his back."

"How on earth did he stand the pain?" William asked.

"He liked to say that he wore his teeth down to the gums from gritting them so much," Fargo said. Neither of them so much as cracked a smile, proving once again that frontier humor was wasted on those who were city bred. Knuckling to the task at hand, he pried at the muscles caught on the point, easing them off a strand at a time. It was a painstaking job, since a single slip would sever the sinew. After what seemed like an hour, Fargo straightened with the arrow in his hand. "There you go," he said, and sat. "Do you want it for a keepsake?"

Melissa sniffed. "Has anyone ever told you that you're not quite right in the head?" She snatched the shaft, broke it over her knee, and threw it. "The only thing I want to remember about this whole expedition is the sight of your back when we part company for good."

Fargo sighed. Everything was back to normal.

They covered the wound with a fresh bandage. Davina stirred when Melissa tied it. She groaned lightly as she opened her eyes, and the first words out of her mouth were, "The damn arrow?"

"Tall, broad, and brainless took it out," Melissa said. "He thought you might want it as a memento," she threw in sarcastically.

"I would," the redhead said. "It will be something to show my kids one day."

Melissa puffed out her lips. "Oh, hell," she complained, rising. "You're worse than he is." Scowling at Fargo, she walked into the high grass to find the pieces.

For several hours they lingered there, until Fargo insisted they head out again. He felt it best to put as many miles as they could between them and the village before dark. Nightfall found them in a sheltered ravine, where their fire could not be seen. For the redhead's sake, Fargo trimmed one end of a long, straight limb and went hunting. He had learned to use a lance during his days with the Sioux, and in short order he had a rabbit roasting on a stick.

"Wouldn't it have been easier to use your gun?" William asked.

"Easier, but a lot louder," Fargo said.

Until dawn they took turns standing guard, except for Davina who slept fitfully. When her father checked on her at first light, he declared, "She has a high fever! Do you think those savages used a poison arrow?"

Fargo doubted it. Although some tribes liked to dip their arrowheads in rattlesnake venom or the bodies of dead animals, the bone point had not been discolored. He cut a strip off of one of his blankets to make a compress, which he soaked in the stream. Davina awakened as he pressed it to her brow. Her pupils, he noticed, were dilated.

"My big protector. What did you do? Set me on fire while I was asleep?"

Melissa leaned over her. "You have a high temperature, sis. But don't you fret. We'll have you back on your feet in no time."

The redhead grinned. "This is a hell of a note. I'm up to my neck in nursemaids." She drifted off once more.

"Can we remain here all day?" William wanted to know.

"It wouldn't be safe," Fargo replied.

The day passed quickly. They stopped whenever they came to a stream to wet Davina's compress and dress her wound. For their midday meal they ate sparingly of the pemmican and jerky. Fargo was pleased with their progress. He traveled due southwest in order to reach the Columbia as close to Portland as possible. That night Davina's fever worsened. Melissa stayed up with her most of the night and was so tired she could barely stay awake the next day.

Fargo did not let on, but he was worried about the redhead. More trappers and mountain men had died from infections brought on by arrow wounds than had died from the arrows themselves. If Davina's wound festered, saving her might be impossible. Which made him all the more glad when her fever broke about thirty hours later. She was as week as an hour-old kitten, but she would live.

It took them almost three days longer to return to the Columbia River than it had taken them to reach Mount Saint Helens. When at last they drew rein on the crown of a hillock and saw the mighty waterway below them, William Nuttall let out a whoop of joy while Melissa clapped her hands with glee. Davina was still too weak to do much more than smile and say, "I've never been so happy to see anything in my life."

Fargo had brought them out of the wilderness within a few hundred yards of where they needed to be. Directly across from Portland lay a sheltered inlet. It was here the ferry operator would come to pick them up once they built a bonfire to signal him.

Since it was late afternoon, Fargo knew they had to get the fire going quickly or forget about crossing until morning. Due to the swift current and treacherous shoreline, the ferryman did not operate at night.

On reaching the flat basin that formed the inlet, Fargo eased Davina to the ground, then slid off and stretched. The redhead leaned on the Ovaro and nodded at the buildings on the south side. "Do you suppose I'll be able to rustle up a bath over there?"

Fargo had been to Portland before. As he recollected, there was one establishment that rented wooden tubs by the hour, but before he could inform the redhead, he saw her gaze go past him and her eyes narrow. Pivoting, he spotted a small tent that had been pitched in the shadow of dense pines close to the basin. Smoke curled from a campfire. A coffeepot sat on a flat stone. Nearer the tent, on a log, rested a tin plate crammed with biscuits.

"Help me over there, Skye," Davina said. "I'd die for a hot cup of coffee."

"You can have it," Melissa said. "I want some of those biscuits. We haven't had a decent meal in ages." She smirked at Fargo. "No offense meant, barbarian. But rabbit meat day in and day out can get tiresome after a while."

William walked toward the tent, cupping a hand to his mouth. "Hello there! Do you mind sharing some of your food with four starved strangers?"

No one answered. No one came out of the tent. Fargo did not see anything wrong with that. He assumed the tent's owner had gone into the brush and would be back shortly. Holding Davina's elbow, ready to grab her if she fell, he followed Melissa and their father.

"Is anyone here?" William hollered. "You have company." He stepped to the flap and peeked inside. "No one," he said. "Now where could they have gotten to?"

"Right here, jackass," grated a rough voice, and two men dressed in seafaring clothes strolled into the open with cocked revolvers leveled. The leaner of the pair snickered. "Look at these jokers, Frank! They don't know what to think."

The Nuttalls were flabbergasted. Fargo studied the faces of the pair and realized that he had seen them before. They were two of the three men who had boarded the *Celeste* right before the clipper ship set sail from San Francisco.

William Nuttall showed some backbone. "Who are you men?" he demanded. "What is the meaning of this outrage? All we want is to share your food. You have no call to be pointing guns at anyone."

"That's where you're wrong, pilgrim," said the lean seaman. "For ten thousand dollars I'd point a gun at my own mother. Then pull the trigger."

The one called Frank chuckled. "Ain't that the truth, Webb." He wagged his revolver at Fargo. "Cat got your tongue, mister?"

William looked at Fargo. "What does he mean? Do you know these two ruffians? What are they up to?"

Fargo released Davina and sidled to the right to spare her from being caught in the cross fire when he went for his gun. But as soon as he began to move, Frank seized Melissa by the arm and jammed the muzzle of his Remington against her head.

"If you so much as twitch, mister, the lady here grows two new ear holes." Frank gouged the barrel into her temple to stress his point. She tried to draw away and he shook her as a terrier might shake a rat, snarling, "Stand still, bitch, or I'll blow out your wick right now."

Webb shoved the artist aside, strode up to Fargo, and plucked the Colt from its holster. Stepping to the left, he wedged it under his belt. "Thanks for the new hardware, friend. A man in my line of work can always use another gun."

William was fit to be tied. "What line of work? Will someone please tell me what is going on?"

Frank nodded at Fargo. "He'll tell you. That is, if he has it figured out yet."

Fargo believed he did, or at least most of it. "Someone sent you and your two friends to kill me because I killed Bruno Scaglia. One of you tried on the *Celeste*. Then you two must have heard Nuttall talk to Captain Gibson about being picked up here. You had Gibson put you off in Portland and hired a boat to bring you over. You've been waiting for us ever since."

Webb uttered a dry, mocking cackle. "Not bad, big man.

You're just a little off the mark. The gent who hired us is Lou Nelson—"

"I don't know anyone by that name," Fargo interrupted. "Was he one of Bruno's men at the gambling hall?"

"I wouldn't know anything about that," Webb said. "Nelson was Bruno's right-hand man. He was at the club the night you opened Scaglia's jugular. Before Bruno died, he made Nelson promise to hunt you down and pay you back."

"That's where we came in," Frank took up the tale. "We're not really sailors. We kill people for a living. For money."

"A lot of money," Webb amended.

Fargo gauged the distance to each killer. He might be able to reach Webb before either of them got off a shot, but Frank would gun him down a moment later.

"As for Captain Gibson," the lean killer said, "he dropped us off right here, not over in Portland." Webb chortled. "I'll bet you didn't know that Gibson used to do some smuggling on the side for Scaglia. That's why Gibson let us pretend to be part of his crew."

Frank had lowered his Remington an inch or so, but it still pointed at Melissa's head. "The old bastard drew the line at murder, though. He made us promise not to try anything until he had put you off his stinking ship. Our friend Hank decided not to wait. Gibson kept us in our cabin after that, but I snuck out and tried to gun you down in the hold."

It all fit, Fargo mused. From how the captain had acted after the attempt on his life to the warning Gibson had given him. "It's me you want," he said. "Why not let these others go?"

"Oh, please," Frank replied. "You know better."

Webb extended his arm and slowly cocked his pistol. "Any last words, mister, before I decorate the grass with you brains?"

Fargo tensed to make a futile leap. His long string of luck had finally played out, but he was not about to go down without a fight.

Just then, to everyone's surprise, Davina Nuttall cried out and shuffled between Fargo and the gunman, weakly waving her arms. "No! You can't! I won't let you murder the man I love!"

William and Melissa were too stunned to speak. They stood there gaping, William with a hand over his heart.

Webb hefted his pistol and barked, "Get the hell out of the way, lady, or I'll do you first."

"Please!" Davina pleaded, her voice husky with emotion. "He means everything to me! Let me hold him once before we die! Is that too much to ask?"

Fargo realized what she was up to and waited for the words that meant life or death to him.

Frank found her request amusing. He glanced at his partner. "I say let the lady have her fun. After she's done holding him, we'll let her take turns holding us for a while."

Webb liked the idea and said so. "If she's real nice, I might even let her hold me all night. You can have the other one. I've always been partial to red hair."

Her head bowed as if in gratitude, Davina turned. She opened her arms wide, then looked up, a grin creasing her face from ear to ear. "Hold me, lover," she said, somehow sounding as if she were about to burst into tears. "Hold me close."

Fargo did. He took a single step and slipped his arms inside her coat as if to embrace her. His hands closed on the smooth butts of her short-barreled, nickel-plated Colts and he paused to say sincerely, "I've never known a woman quite like you before." Then he bent, pretending to kiss her even as he drew the pistols.

"Hold it! I've changed my mind," Frank declared, leering. "I was just toying with you. Move out of the way, lady. You're all ours from here on out."

Davina glanced at him and smiled ever so sweetly. "You wish, you stupid son of a bitch."

Fargo was in motion before the words were out of her mouth. He stepped to the right and fired both Colts from the hip. One slug cored Frank's head, blowing out the back of his cranium and spinning him around like a child's top. He was dead on his feet, but he still tried to point his revolver. Life faded from his eyes as he melted to the ground.

Webb had been hit in the shoulder. The impact jolted him, but he caught himself and went to shoot.

Fargo fired again, both pistols thundering as one, not once but three times. The lean killer was hurled backward, tripped over the log, and thudded to the earth with his arms and legs twitching. The man gurgled, flailed the air, and died.

"My God!" William exclaimed.

Fargo stared at the Colts, twirled them so the grips were to the front, and held them out to the redhead. "I'm obliged," he said simply.

"Anytime, handsome." Davina raised one pistol, blew at the smoke curling from the end of the barrel, then winked. "Anytime at all."

LOOKING FORWARD!
The following is the opening section from the next novel in the exciting *Trailsman* series from Signet:

THE TRAILSMAN #174
DEATH VALLEY BLOODBATH

1861, Death Valley—
a fitting name for a
living hell, where death
was always a heartbeat away . . .

Skye Fargo knew the ways of the wilderness better than most men. He had learned many valuable lessons while roaming the West from end to end, and one of the most important had to be that a wise man always rode the high lines when in rough country.

It was plain common sense. Travelers who failed to spot trouble coming paid for their mistake with their lives. Many an unwary rider had fallen prey to hostiles, bad men, or beasts, and Fargo did not intend to be one of them.

On this particular day, the big man with the intense lake-blue eyes was riding northeast from Los Angeles. He intended to follow the Sierra Nevadas north to a pass that would take him on into Nevada Territory. It was a trek he had made several times, but even though he knew the lay of the land well, he took no chances. He rode alert at all times, his right hand resting on his thigh within inches of his polished Colt.

A blazing sun had the sky all to itself. Many kinds of colorful birds sang gaily or flitted in the trees. Squirrels and chipmunks frolicked everywhere. On occasion, solitary hawks wheeled high overhead. Less frequently, majestic eagles did the same. Several times since dawn Fargo had spooked deer, and he looked forward to treating himself to a juicy venison steak for supper.

At the sight of a plume of gray smoke, Fargo reined up. So far as he knew, there were no homesteads in that region. Nor were there likely to be anytime soon. Settling there was too risky, since just over the range lay sprawling desert country, home to the fierce Mohave Indians. Wondering if he might have stumbled on a roving band, he rose in the stirrups.

The switchback Fargo was descending wound into a small valley watered by a narrow stream. Someone was down there in a stand of trees on the south bank. Judging by the large amount of smoke, Fargo doubted Indians were to blame. Every frontiersman worthy of the name knew that Indians kept their fires small.

Fargo had no hankering for company. He'd had his share in Los Angeles, having spent a whole week playing poker and dallying with a frisky dove. Besides, he was due in Salt Lake City by the end of the month. So, going on, he came to the valley floor and swung to the right to skirt the stand. He could hear low voices but not distinct words. A horse nickered.

Hugging the tree line, Fargo held the pinto stallion to a walk. He kept one eye on the cottonwoods and spied several figures moving about. When he was almost abreast of them, a glimmer of long blond hair told him a woman was with the group, and he relaxed a bit. Few females rode with outlaw gangs. He cocked his head to see her better, then froze as the metallic rasp of a rifle lever warned him that he had let his curiosity get the better of him.

"Hold up there, mister! And keep those hands where I can see 'em."

To argue invited a bullet. Fargo reluctantly did as the hombre wanted, hiking his arms to show his peaceful intentions. "I'm not looking for trouble," he stressed.

"Who the hell cares?"

The brush parted, revealing a grizzled hard case in buckskins similar to Fargo's, except his were caked with grease and grime from top to bottom. A sparse salt-and-pepper beard covered his lower jaw. He wore a grin, which didn't fit with the cocked Spencer in his weathered hands.

"I don't like having guns pointed at me," Fargo mentioned calmly enough, given that he wanted to take the Spencer and wrap it around the man's scrawny neck.

"Then maybe you shouldn't go sneakin' around the way you do," the hard case responded. Moving warily around the front of the stallion, he trained the rifle on Fargo's chest, then tossed back his head and hollered. "Clem! Trench! We got us some company!"

The cry brought a half-dozen others from the stand. Foremost among them was the blonde, a shapely woman who carried herself as if she owned the world. Narrowed green eyes studied the Trailsman as she approached. A riding outfit clothed her lush form, doing ample justice to the enticing swell of her bosom and the inviting sway of her hips. From the neck down she was all soft curves and cleavage, but from the neck up she was as hard as flint. She had a jutting jaw, high cheekbones, and all the warmth of a glacier in her stare.

Beside her stalked a tall man wearing a pair of ivory-handled Colts, slung low. A wide-brimmed black hat crowned a square head perched on broad shoulders. He had big hands, the thumbs hooked in his black gun belt. His vest, pants, and boots were also black. Large Spanish-style spurs jingled with every step.

"What do we have here, Otis?" the woman said, halting. In her right hand was a thick quirt, which she tapped against her left palm.

"I caught 'im tryin' to sneak on by us," the old man declared.

Fargo was taking his measure of the others. They all had the mean look of human vultures, of men who lived by their guns and their brawn.

"Is that true?" the woman asked.

There was no reason for Fargo to answer. He had done nothing wrong and they knew it. Whatever they were up to, they would show their colors soon enough. His only regret was that he had been harebrained enough to get caught.

The tall gent with fancy hardware stepped forward. "Didn't you hear the lady, friend? She asked you a question. You'll answer her, if you know what's good for you."

Bending, Fargo made a show of examining the man's bull neck.

"What the hell are you doing?"

"Looking for the leash," Fargo responded.

The woman grinned, the man called Otis chuckled, and the tall man in the black hat scowled. Suddenly, brawny hands clamped on Fargo's shirt. He was lifted clear off the saddle and heaved into the grass. Rolling as he hit, Fargo rose into a crouch, ready to defend himself despite the ring of pistols that had blossomed in the hands of the rest.

The blonde moved, smacking her quirt against the tall gunman's chest. "That's enough! And the same goes for all of you! There will be no gunplay unless I give the word. Savvy?"

No one debated the point, so the woman turned and bestowed a smile on Fargo. "Riling Dee Trench isn't the smartest thing in the world to do, mister. He's killed men for a lot less. Once, he shot a gent for looking crosswise at him."

Fargo slowly uncoiled, careful not to lower his hand too near his revolver. The smart thing to do was to go easy, to put a rein on his temper, to hear them out. But he couldn't help himself. "Was the man facing him at the time?"

Trench bristled. His fingers formed into claws. He resembled a bear about to pounce, but at a sharp glance from the woman he held himself in check and slowly let the tension drain away.

"Keep it up, mister," the woman said, "and I won't be responsible for what happens. I'm trying to do you a favor, but you act as if you want to commit suicide."

Fargo nodded at Otis's Spencer. "You call holding a man at gunpoint doing him a favor? Most people would call that being mighty impolite."

The woman walked up to him. Her luxurious hair gave off a minty fragrance that competed with the alluring perfume she favored. Her full lips quirked upward. "Another time and place, and I'd find your sense of humor refreshing. As it is, I'm afraid I have to put business before pleasure." She paused. "What's your name?"

Fargo deliberately stared at her chest. The way her twin peaks pushed against the fabric, it was a miracle she didn't burst from her blouse like an overripe melon. "I don't see any badge," he told her.

Otis snickered. "Uppity cuss, ain't he, Miss Langtree?" He squinted at Fargo. "For your information, mister, we don't need no stinkin' badges. In case you can't count, there's eight of us and only one of you. So you'd best loosen them lips of yours, pronto."

Langtree shushed him with a gesture, then placed her warm hand on Fargo's wrist. "We have no call to snip at each other like this. I'm sure that once you understand, you'll cooperate."

"Don't hold your breath."

Dee Trench took a step, but again the beautiful woman exercised her remarkable control and rooted him in place with a bob of her fine head.

"Now then," she said, taking gentle hold of Fargo's fingers, "why don't we start this whole business over again, and do it right? I'm Veronica Langtree. I operate a gambling hall in Los Angeles. Perhaps you've heard of it? The Lucky Lady?"

Fargo was impressed. The Lucky Lady had a justly deserved reputation as being the finest establishment of its kind south of San Francisco. Chandeliers, thick burgundy carpet, and mahogany furniture testified to the quality of its clientele. He had visited it once, but the stakes had proven too high for his poke. "You're a long way from home," he commented.

"With good cause," Langtree said. "I'm after a skunk who cheated one of my new dealers out of over ten thousand dollars last week, and I don't aim to rest until he's made good the money."

The story was plausible. Casinos and saloons never tolerated cheats and swindlers, unless they were on the payroll of the house. Professional gamblers knew better than to ply their trade in a first-rate place like the Lucky Lady, where they were more likely to be caught. And more likely to lose a few fingers or teeth as a warning to others.

"He's hiding out in this area?" Fargo asked.

"No, the worm *lives* in this neck of the woods. He's an old prospector by the name of Luke Gantry. Twice a year or so he strays down into Los Angeles to buy supplies and treat himself to a night on the town. This time he just happened to pick my place." Langtree scowled. "He's going to learn the hard way that no one cheats me and lives to brag about it."

It was common knowledge that dealers at joints like the Lucky Lady were the best gamblers in the business. So it seemed strange to Fargo that an ordinary prospector had outwitted one. "You say this Gantry fleeced your man?"

"With one of the oldest tricks in the book. A mirror ring."

Fargo was familiar with the trick. A cardsharp would buy an ordinary finger ring with a flat surface on the band and polish the surface until it gleamed like a mirror. With it, a man could read all the cards being dealt. Plenty had been hung for using them.

"A friend of Gantry's told on him," the woman went on, and sighed. "I was gone the night Luke stopped by, which is a shame. I would have been suspicious right away. Gantry never won that much money at one time in his whole life. If I'd been there and had him searched, I could have saved myself a lot of trouble."

The blonde sounded sincere, yet at the back of Fargo's mind gnawed a pinprick of doubt. "If you know who you're after, why stop me?" he asked innocently enough while taking a step to his right, which put him closer to the Ovaro and within an arm's length of Otis and that unwavering Spencer. Most of the other gunmen had let their guard down and were not covering him as carefully as they should.

"Because Gantry's shack is too well hidden. We know the general area where to find it, but we could search for a month of Sundays and never hit pay dirt," Langtree said. "He has friends, though, who come out to visit him from time to time. I'm hoping we can persuade one of them to tell us where it is."

Again something did not quite ring true, but Fargo had no time to figure it out.

Trench cut in, snapping, "That someone is you, jackass. Tell us while you have your teeth."

"I don't know any Luke Gantry," Fargo declared. He had to lull them into thinking he had no intention of bucking them, so he smiled, adding, "And it seems to me that you're going about this all wrong. If I were Gantry, I wouldn't hang around. He's probably halfway to St. Louis by now." Another short step put him right where he wanted to be.

Veronica shook her head. "You don't know that old cuss like I do. Gantry will never leave here. He loves it too much."

Otis finally let the barrel of the Spencer dip. Not more than an inch, but it was enough.

The moment Skye Fargo had been waiting for had come. Keeping his tone casual, he remarked, "I haven't seen anyone since I left the coast. Unless you count those Indians this morning."

Every last one of them was intensely interested. Langtree stiffened. "What Indians? Were they Mohaves?"

"I couldn't say," Fargo said, shifting to point to the south. "They were just past that sawtooth ridge on the horizon."

It was one of the oldest ploys around. Fargo hadn't encountered any hostiles. His sole purpose was to distract Langtree and her bunch, to get them to focus on that ridge for a few seconds instead of on him. And it worked better than he had dared hope. Every last one of them turned to study the landmark. The instant they did, Fargo exploded into action. Grabbing the Spencer's muzzle, he wrenched it from Otis's grasp, even as he swiveled to slam the stock into the temple of the nearest gun shark. The rifle went off, the slug catching yet another hard case in the shoulder and knocking the man to the ground.

Much too late, Langtree's men realized their mistake. They started to bring up their pistols. Dee Trench went for his, his brawny hands a blur, his draw smooth and graceful, like the striking of twin rattlesnakes. But in this case he was not nearly fast enough.

Skye Fargo only had to pivot to plant a boot in Trench's groin. At the same time, his own Colt cleared leather. It was cocked and extended and touching Veronica Langtree's brow before the others could cover him. "Anyone moves and she dies," he barked.

To a man, they froze. Except for Trench, who had sagged to his knees with his hands over his manhood and was sputtering and wheezing like a busted bellows, and the wounded gunman, who thrashed on the ground with a palm pressed to his bleeding shoulder.

The blonde, to Fargo's surprise, displayed no fear. She stood there with her head held high and a hint of a smile curling those luscious lips.

The youngest of her hired help, a thin kid with pimples and a derby, kept glancing back and forth between Fargo and his employer. "You're bluffing, stranger," he said. "You ain't about to shoot a lady in cold blood."

It was Otis who answered. "Crespin! You lower that iron

right this second, or so help me, when this is over I'll skin you alive and make you eat your oysters, to boot!"

Veronica spoke. "You heard Otis. I want all of you to do exactly as this gentleman tells you to do. There will be no heroics. Is that understood?"

Fargo seized the advantage while he had it. "Shuck the shells from those cylinders, boys. Then toss the artillery into the grass. And be quick about it."

While they complied, Langtree eyed Fargo from head to toe, then commented, "You know, mister, there's more to you than I thought. I haven't met anyone with your kind of grit in a long time."

"You like men who hold guns to your pretty head?"

"I like a real *man*. And it seems they're getting harder to find all the time." Langtree glanced down at Dee Trench. "He tries hard, but he's rough around the edges yet."

Fargo honestly didn't know whether to laugh in her face or feel flattered. He watched her underlings closely, and when the last revolver went flying, he lowered his pistol but held it pointed at her stomach, just in case. Stepping to Trench, he plucked both expensive Colts from their silver-inlaid holsters and tossed them, then did the same with the wounded gunman's .36-caliber Navy. Wagging his gun, he had Otis, Crespin, and the rest move away from the Ovaro, giving him room to mount.

Trench had stopped sputtering but still was unable to straighten. Glaring, he growled, "We'll meet again one day, bastard. When we do, I'll make you eat that boot."

"Then you might as well make me eat both, since they're a set," Fargo said. Without warning, he kicked the gunfighter flush in the mouth with is other foot. Trench crumpled, bleeding profusely from a split lower lip.

"Son of a bitch!" one of the men blurted.

Fargo wasn't done yet. Whirling, he strode over to Otis. "As for you, mister," he said, and drove the Colt into the other man's gut, doubling Otis over, "the next time someone tells you they don't like having a rifle pointed at them, maybe you'll listen."

If looks could kill, Fargo would have been blasted to tiny pieces as he backpedaled to the stallion and gripped the saddle horn. Only Veronica Langtree showed no anger or resentment. Oddly enough, her gaze held newfound respect. Fargo hooked a stirrup, then eased into the creaking saddle. "I don't want to see anyone on my back trail."

No one had anything to say.

Lightly applying his spurs, Fargo walked the pinto backward in order to keep Langtree and her hired cutthroats in front of him until he gained the cover of the forest. It was a trick he had taught the stallion long ago, one that had saved his hide time and again. Langtree grinned and waved as the foliage closed around them.

The moment the vegetation screened him, Skye Fargo wheeled his mount and sped at a gallop to the east. His shoulders prickled for over half a mile. He half expected to hear gunfire and see the gunmen hot on his trail. But they never appeared. Only after an hour had gone by was he willing to take it for granted that he had given them the slip.

Fargo was glad to be shy of Veronica Langtree. She was trouble, the kind of person who did as she damn well pleased when she damn well pleased, without any regard for the consequences. If he had to guess, he'd say her beauty hid a heart as cold and calculating as any man's. He had met her kind before and always regretted getting involved with them. No, sir, he reflected. Give him an easygoing saloon girl any day.

The bright sun and abundant wildlife soon took Fargo's mind off the encounter. Presently he spied a long valley to the east and beyond it the Inyo Mountains. Thanks to the blonde and her men, he had strayed much farther west than he originally intended. It was high time to swing to the north again and make for the high pass over the Sierras.

By now Fargo was well up in the high country. He angled across a verdant meadow, scattering butterflies and scaring a pair of grouse into taking wing. Farther on he came to a steep ravine and bore eastward along the rim in search of a trail to the opposite side that would be easy on the Ovaro. Idly, he stretched, and as he did, he happened to glance back the way he had come. Perhaps a quarter of a mile away, sunlight glinted off metal.

Fargo's features hardened. He'd warned Langtree and she hadn't listened, so whatever happened next was on her shoulders. Veering into the pines, he yanked the heavy Henry from its saddle scabbard, worked the lever to feed a .44-caliber round into the chamber, and halted in the shadows. Whoever Langtree had sent was about to learn that trying to bushwhack him was a surefire invitation to an early grave.

It wasn't long before the rider appeared, a stick figure hundreds of yards distant. To Fargo's amazement, the man rode right out in the open, making no attempt at all to conceal himself. Fargo suspected it must be the pimply kid, Crespin. None of the others had struck him as being that stupid.

A minute went by, and Fargo grew puzzled. The rider wasn't sticking to his trail. Instead, the man weaved all over the place, first to the right, then to the left, then straight for a dozen feet before meandering off again. Fargo had no idea what to make of the rider's bizarre antics, unless Crespin had lost the Ovaro's tracks and was hunting for them again. But that couldn't be. The prints were so fresh, a five-year-old could follow them with ease.

Fargo pressed the rifle stock to his right shoulder, took a bead on the rider, and waited for the man's chest to fill the sights. Which didn't happen. The rider appeared to be bent low over the saddle, evidently examining the ground. As the horse drew nearer, Fargo saw that he was mistaken. The man wasn't bent low—he hung limply, facedown, both arms dangling, still and lifeless.

Wary of being lured into the gun sights of other men lurking back in the trees, Fargo replaced the Henry and let the sorrel get close to the ravine before he burst from cover. The sorrel nickered and turned to flee, but the stallion was on it before it could. Fargo caught hold of the bridle, bringing the skittish animal to a stop.

The rider had one leg crooked over the saddle horn, the other snagged in a stirrup. It explained why he was still in the saddle. A broad brown hat secured by a chin strap concealed most of his face.

Fargo dismounted. Stroking the sorrel to calm it, he edged to the slumped form. A dark stain high on the man's back framed a bullet hole. Whoever it was had been ambushed, shot from behind. Fargo worked the snagged boot back and forth until it slipped free. Reaching up, he straightened the crooked leg and had to brace himself as the body slid off into his arms. The hat fell, cascading rich black hair across his broad shoulders. At the same instant, he felt large, soft breasts under his forearm. Startled, he found himself nose to nose with an incredibly beautiful woman.

Dark eyes snapped wide. They held a hint of panic, which was promptly replaced by simmering rage. "I'll kill you!" she screeched. Spearing her hands at his face, she clawed at his eyes like a wildcat gone berserk.

WHISPERS OF THE RIVER
BY TOM HRON

They came from an Old West no longer wild and free—lured by tales of a fabulous gold strike in Alaska. They found a land of majestic beauty, but one more brutal than hell. Some found wealth beyond their wildest dreams, but most suffered death and despair. With this rush of brawling, lusting, striving humanity, walked Eli Bonnet, a legendary lawman who dealt out justice with his gun ... and Hannah Twigg, a woman who dared death for love and everything for freedom. A magnificent saga filled with all the pain and glory of the Yukon's golden days....

from **SIGNET**

FALCONER'S LAW
BY JASON MANNING

The year is 1837. The fur harvest that bred a generation of dauntless, daring mountain men is growing smaller. The only way for them to survive is the way westward, across the cruelest desert in the West, over the savage mountains, through hostile Indian territory, to a California of wealth, women, wine, and ruthless Mexican authorities.

Only one man can meet that brutal challenge—His name is Hugh Falconer—and his law is that of survival. . . .

from **SIGNET**

Prices slightly higher in Canada.   (0-451-18645-1—$5.50)